One Drop
Holds The Sun

GW00771953

One Drop Holds The Sun

This book is the result of a series of creative writing workshops run for birth mothers attending BEAM. The workshops were run weekly online, facilitated by writer, Helen Jacey, and were focused on the theme of travel and adventure.

The workshops and the book were supported using public funding by the National Lottery through Arts Council England.

About BEAM

BEAM is a charity that provides peer to peer support for birth mothers apart from their children. We provide online and face to face meetings as well as training for professionals.

Contact BEAM

If you would like to connect with BEAM, email us
hello@beam.support
or call us
01473 760800

www.beam.support

"Humanity flows from stories that make meaning. These stories offer a rare, raw but beautiful attempt to reconcile life's highest price – to lose a child. A should-read for all families and professionals involved in child protection. We should thank these creative women for demanding our care and compassion through their stories and their determination to heal."
Mike Blows, Child and Family Psychiatrist & Expert Witness

"*One Drop Holds the Sun* is a raw, emotional, and compelling account of loss, grief, guilt, and hope. Through the eyes of Hope, a mother whose children have been removed from her care by Social Services, we witness the family court system and Social Services in unflinching detail. What unfolds is terrifying, shocking, and maddening. This is a must-read for every parent and every professional working in Family Law."
Sonia Simms, Barrister & Founder of AdvocacyTutor.com

"This is not just a story of trauma, loss, shame and despair but one of love, healing and Hope. The interweaving of fantasy, imagination and creativity with the authentic voice of experience creates a compelling narrative with many moments that hit hard in the heart of the reader."
Juliet Kesteven, Consultant Social Work Supervisor and Trainer at Cambridge Centre for Attachment

"A raw and transparent insight into what it feels like to somehow have to find the will to keep going when your heart has been ripped apart. It bears witness to, and gives voice to women whose voices have gone unheard or been ignored, dismissed or not believed. While it does not shy

away from the trauma and pain the women have all experienced it offers a genuine sense of Hope – embodied in the character of Hope and her journey towards the acceptance of what has happened and the way she moves beyond her hurt and pain to finding a way to build a life where she is fulfilled and finds meaning. What shines through all the stories is the importance of community; supporting, encouraging and helping each other to keep on going in the most difficult of circumstances – the very essence of what BEAM stands for."
Shuna McCahon, Counsellor & Co-founder BEAM

"This compelling and imaginative story shines a light on the hidden, heartbreaking reality of a mother whose children have been removed from her care. Hope is a character who is often vilified and forgotten by society, but One Drop Can Hold the Sun ensures the reader remembers the humanity of these women. It is essential reading for any healthcare professional who works with women and families and I commend the bravery and vision of the women who authored it.
Catherine Cracknell, Specialist Midwife

Dedicated to

Emma & all the BEAM mums
who felt they were the only ones

&

to Helen

for her kindness and inspiration in teaching us
how to become the writers we never knew we would be

Acknowledgements

Supported using public funding by the National Lottery through Arts Council.

We are grateful to the charity, Kintsugi Hope, for the support and care they provide to those who face challenges in their mental health. The encouragement they have given to us as a charity is greatly appreciated.

BEAM would not be the amazing charity it is without the wonderful kindness and generosity of our volunteers and donors. You have given so much to us and we are forever indebted to you. We especially wish to acknowledge Janice, who continued to help run the Carry On BEAMing group despite living in another country and her ballet training!

Last but not least, to Paula and everyone at the Haven Project Liverpool for the encouragement and determination to love and never give up!

Psalm 139

One Drop
Holds The Sun

by
BEAM

Alex, Cat, Cherie, Cheryl, Dani, Donna,
Elina, Gianina, Janice, Kye, Marie, Nat,
Natty, Penny, Rachel, Shelly, Tasha, Tracey

First published 2024
By BEAM
Address: 1 Chapel Cottage, Upper Street, Witnesham IP6 9ER
© Beam 2024

This is a work of fiction. All of the characters in this book are fictional and any resemblance to an actual person is coincidental. Names, organisations, places, and events are either products of the authors' imaginations or used fictitiously.
All rights reserved. No part of this book may be reprinted or reproduced or utilised in any form or by any electronic, mechanical, or other means, now known or hereafter invented, including photocopying and recording, or in any information storage or retrieval system, without permission in writing from the publishers.

BEAM is a registered charity number 1187918
♥ BEAM
Cover Image and illustrations by Alex.
Cover design by Cassia Friello of Tesoro Creative Ltd.
Typesetting by Elaine Sharples.

ISBN: (pbk) 978-1-0369-0360-2

Introduction by Helen Jacey,
creative writing workshop facilitator

Where would you go, what world would you create, if you could go anywhere?

This was the question the mothers, volunteers and BEAM trustees and I explored in a series of weekly online creative writing workshops in 2024. Through written words, imagination, and the sharing of ideas, the worlds that the participants created were as individual, colourful and vibrant as they are.

From the Roman Empire to the 2030s via an English Victorian farm and seventeenth century Ashanti Kingdom, we time-travelled to others' stories, amazed at the ways we could meet new characters and discover new places in the creative process.

Each participant crafted adventure stories that were important to them. My role was to facilitate, inspire and support their creativity and confidence in writing. More often than not I felt the group's openness and their heartfelt encouragement of one another were the real facilitators, ones that taught so much to me.

It was at the end of our planned sessions that the group decided that their individual stories could be joined together, by means of a central character, a young woman who had lost care of her children. As part of her journey to healing and her seemingly impossible task of coming to terms with her loss, this woman could time-travel to all their stories.

The group brainstormed what had happened to her, what she was like, and what could happen to her in the future. Together, they created a vulnerable woman whose heart was broken, and who didn't know a way forward. A BEAM volunteer trustee with knowledge of child protection would write Hope's storyline.

I was deeply touched when the mums asked me to name her. A name instantly leapt out to me.

Hope.

The group approved of this name choice.

We then decided it would be up to each writer to decide how Hope would enter their story. Maybe their character would just have a short but meaningful interaction with Hope. Maybe Hope would play a bigger role.

Every story reveals a powerful transaction between Hope and the characters she meets. These interactions reveal care, compassion and empathy, and offer ways of learning and growing.

Each story reflects what Hope needs on her journey of healing.

In this way, each writer has made a unique choice about Hope that reflects the message of their story and how they wanted to write their story. Accordingly, some stories are narrated by a different character, in the first person, some are third person. Sometimes Hope appears early in the story, sometimes later.

Beam members have also contributed to the book through their poems, drawings, letters, other writing or feedback. Each contribution reflects the diversity of voices in creating Hope's journey.

As you read the book, please see the stories, poems and pictures as a tapestry of ideas and contributions, woven together to make a whole.

A shared hope for the book was that it would help others going through similar circumstances. It could also assist professionals involved in childcare proceedings develop more empathy for parents who lose their children, and highlight how parents often don't get the support when they need it, to enable them to keep their children.

Together, the words and images share one core theme, that healing and recovery is a journey, and one that is always better shared.

Chapter 1

Present Day

Most people look out the window for a reason. What's the weather like? Who is making that unearthly noise? Is my bike still there? But others just need to see something, anything outside their four walls.

There is a plastic chair by the bay window with a young woman in it. Her arms resting on the windowsill, her head resting on her arms. She has been there for an hour now. The shadows under her eyes have grown darker but the sun is rising. How can a twenty-seven year old have such a lined face? She is crying, unable to even talk to herself. Her name is Hope.

Hope is in her bedroom wearing some old faded blue jeans, a red t-shirt which has seen better days and a black hoodie with a picture of the Colosseum on the back. It says *ROMAN GODDESS* on the front.

The weather is dull and wet, an echo of what is within.

It is a noise that makes her lift her heavy head that day to look out of the grubby window. Like a fluttering of sifted flour sprinkling softly into a large, glass bowl. It was indistinct, that soft pattering, but it is only more rain. Why won't it stop raining?

At the family centre where she saw her children, Hope once heard an Afghani woman say how if it ever rained in Kabul, which was rare, she would run to her window, pull back her covered arms and thrust out her hands. She said that if there was a wind it would sometimes blow the wet droplets onto her face. "This make me happy. I like so much this rain," the woman had said. Maybe that's why Hope cherished the sun. It made an all too rare appearance for her liking in Edenton.

It is February 18th, but Hope doesn't know that. The days drift and sometimes seem to have ended before they have begun. It probably isn't relevant that a day has a number when you are simply trying to survive. The numbers that have a meaning to Hope are twenty-seven, her age. She lives at number nine on the second floor of a council flat. She has three children.

She *had* three children.

At times their ages over the years have become muddled in her mind and this makes her feel ashamed. Who forgets how old their children are? Biting her lower lip, she is not going to think about that today. She has a hangover. She swipes the condensation from the window. It acts like a veil shielding her large, hazel eyes from the outside world and everything that is kept away from her.

When she was young, Hope would write her initials in

the mist on the window of the bus. She would then write the initials of the boy she fancied next to them but in a flash rub them out. The letters she would write today would be J, M & A but someone else has rubbed them out without her consent.

Voices disturb her thoughts. There is a group of teenage girls walking fast through the wet streets. Cars line each side of the road. All their wing mirrors are tucked in tight to their sides like a bird ready to dive bomb into the large, dirty puddles. No one wants their mirrors stripped off by a hooligan walking past the flats or a car careering too fast down the narrow road. This street is a cut through to the school. The children pass screeching, yelling and making a racket. It's midday, but the exhaustion takes over again. Hope goes back to bed. She pulls the pillow and duvet over her head to avoid hearing children.

She wakes with a start. Was there movement of the curtain, as if someone was trying to draw it back? Pulling herself out of bed she goes to the window and peers outside. In the distance, a girl runs fast. "She must be late for school," thinks Hope. All the other children have long since passed by; but now it is just this silent, single runner advancing quickly towards her down the narrow road.

Why does Hope imagine the girl is a messenger or a relay runner? Where is the baton that should be gripped tightly in her hand? Who is ahead of her to take hold of it? The girl's dark hair is flying behind her like the wild mane of a stallion, her knees are kicking up as she powers ahead. Suddenly, the runner stops abruptly, right below Hope's window. A book has fallen out of the girl's wet hand. She reaches down swiftly to pick it up.

"I recognise that book!" Hope says to herself. "It's the one about the Roman Empire that I read in Middle school!"

Books were a way of escape when she was a child. But her mind, scattered with lashings of grief and waves of regret, can't focus on the written word. Hope hurriedly wipes a swirl of mist away. She leans in close, gazing down at the girl and the book. The girl turns her head and looks up at the window.

Hope takes a gasp of breath and leans back quickly. Where did the light come from that struck the thousand tiny beads of water covering the window and causing them to shimmer? Her blurry reflection gazes back through the crystals of light in front of her. She blinks repeatedly. She is in a palace...

Chapter 2

Roman Empire 27 AD
Nat's story

How is she in a palace?! Is this a dream?! Where is the girl who had just been straining to see her? Hope has honed a skill at not being seen. But now she finds herself standing in a large corridor of what appears to be a Roman Palace. Shocked and confused about how this has happened. She looks around slowly taking in her surroundings as the huge pillars tower above her head.

But she wasn't the only one feeling confused. It was a hot, humid day in the Roman Empire. Cornelius has begun his day the same way he does every day. First, he washed and dressed in his elegant clothing before entering the great hall for his usual extravagant breakfast, fit only for royalty. Cornelius lives a very lavish life with a lavishly decorated home with servants or slaves to tend to his every need. Today is extra special for Cornelius as it is his birthday. As part of his birthday celebrations, he would normally attend the annual Gladiator fights in the colosseum in the capital of Rome. This is an event Cornelius particularly looks forward to. However, today he doesn't feel like going and he doesn't know why. He heads to the state rooms.

Hope hears something rhythmic gradually growing. It

is like a hushing, brushing sound but evolves into the clear known sound of footsteps. She darts to a pillar but then slowly turns as if doing it slowly will help her not be seen. Her head moves towards the direction the noise is coming from, scared and worried by what is approaching. She puts up the hood of her sweatshirt and tries to disappear behind the marble pillar. She thinks, "I need to hide from whoever is coming."

Just then a tall, dark-haired man appears from behind one of the many columns that surround her. This man appears to be dressed in very elegant attire. He is wearing a long, red gown with gold braiding around it. His strong legs with leather saddles are walking towards her! He appears to be alarmed and shocked to see a stranger standing in his Palace. The man approaches Hope and demands to know, "Who are you and what are you doing in my Palace?"

Hope still thinking she is dreaming, says, "I don't know why I am here or where I am. I thought I was still in my bedroom! Who are you and what are you doing here?"

"I'm Cornelius, the Emperor of the Roman

Empire and you are in my Palace! I demand you explain how you got here! What is your name, Woman?" He stands with his hands on his hips.

"I don't know how I got here. The last thing I remember I was looking out of my bedroom window and the next thing I know I am stood in your Palace. And my name is Hope."

Hope is wary of Cornelius. She recognises that he is a person of significant authority. She is wary because anyone who ever had authority has hurt her. It was authority who took her children away from her, so she struggles to trust anyone with power.

"Please, walk with me and we can talk more."

Hope feels she has no choice but to follow. Cornelius explains that as Hope is a person in a foreign place, he as emperor of the empire, has a duty to protect Hope and help her to move on her way. Hope is uncertain about this but does as she is asked and follows cautiously beside Cornelius. They walk down the corridor past many different enormous doors that lead off numerous other corridors. They finally approach a huge carved door covered in gold. The door is opened by palace staff. Cornelius invites Hope to enter the room. Hope stands in the doorway frozen to the spot. She finds herself in an exquisite room of marble and glass, statues and gold everywhere! In the centre of the room, Hope sees a very long table with many seats surrounding it. She is flabbergasted at the sight of the grandeur she now finds herself standing in.

Bewildered by her surroundings, it takes her time to realise that Cornelius has already taken his seat at the head of the elaborate table and invited her to join him at the place setting next to his. Cautious by this request Hope remains standing in the same spot not entirely sure if she heard Cornelius right. Cornelius addresses Hope this time calling her name to gain her attention.

"Hope, please come and take a seat next to me and we can discuss exactly why you are here and how you got here."

Realising she has heard right, Hope slowly moves towards the place where Cornelius gestured she should sit. She takes her place at the glittering table. There is a crystal wine glass and some elaborate food placed on the table in front of her. Unsure if she is to help herself to the things placed in front of her, she decides to remain still and not touch anything. Inside she is both hungry and thirsty but doesn't want to appear rude and eat the food.

After what seemed like a long time Cornelius again addresses Hope. "Hope, do please feel free to eat. You must be hungry."

"I am but I don't want you to feel like you have to provide me with a meal."

"Hope, please eat, you don't have to wait till you return home. As my guest I invite you to join me for this meal."

"That is very kind of you Cornelius, but only if you are sure?"

"Yes, I am sure, then afterwards we can take a stroll in the gardens, and you can tell me about yourself."

"Ummmm, okay," she says worriedly but then adds, "Thank you." She tucks into the most delicious food she has ever tasted.

"Hope, you are most welcome." Cornelius grins as he

watches her devour her meal.

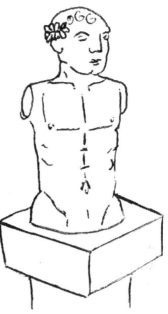

Hope and Cornelius finish their fabulous meal and then make their way outside. The gardens are breath-taking. The flowers and shrubs with fabulous fountains and beautiful manicured lawns all lie before them. Hope spends some time admiring the view. Soon they start walking. Neither say a word. Cornelius then breaks the silence.

"So, Hope, please tell me a bit about yourself."

"Well, I'm not really sure where to begin if I'm totally honest."

"That is okay, Hope, just take your time. It must be hard to tell someone you have only just met about yourself. How about you start by telling me about where you are from and go from there?"

Hope decides that as she is in a dream she won't hold back.

"Ok, well, as you already know my name is Hope and I live in a city called Edenton in England. I had three children. I mean I have three children."

Cornelius looks at her with a piercing gaze leaning in to listen to what she has to say. He doesn't eye her critically. There was a feeling of someone really interested in her as a person.

"I was married to a man called Jimmy but we got divorced. We had two beautiful children together – Jay and Maddison but I call her Maddie. Our relationship was violent and abusive. Someone alerted the police to this after they heard some commotion coming from my home and heard my children crying."

Hope begins to cry. Cornelius places his hand gently on Hope's shoulder which makes Hope jump and pull away. She isn't going to let him touch her.

"Please accept my apologies. I didn't mean to startle you. Take your time, this must be very difficult for you."

"Thanks, it is very hard for me to talk about. The police contacted the local authority because of their concerns for the safety of my children. I did everything I could to try and keep my children in my care, but the local authority refused to allow them to remain with me because they felt I was not in a position to ensure I could keep them safe."

Hope now is sobbing uncontrollably as she tries her best to continue to tell Cornelius her story. "I'm sorry Cornelius, I tried not to cry but it is so, so hard not to. I love my children unconditionally and wouldn't do anything to cause them harm."

"You don't need to apologise Hope, sometimes it helps to have a cry. Take your time, it must be very difficult for you, and I cannot even begin to imagine what you are going through."

"It's extremely hard, I can't actually remember the last time I had a day where I haven't cried. I just want my babies home."

"Who are your children with now?"

"I don't know, all I know is they will remain in the care

of the local authority. The decision was made that the children would remain in care even though I did everything I could do to get them returned to me."

"Oh, Hope! I am so sorry you are having to go through this horrible time in your life. Are you able to see them?"

"Thank you, yes, I did see them during the assessments social services carried out. I was able to see them in a contact centre. A supervisor would watch me and make notes. The hardest part was I would only get two hours every two weeks and it broke my heart every time I had to leave them."

Cornelius can see that Hope has shared as much as she can. "Time is moving on rapidly and I am due to attend an event at the Colosseum in a couple of hours so I must retreat to my quarters and prepare. You are dutifully invited to join me at my event as my guest."

"That is very kind of you Cornelius, but I am not exactly appropriately dressed for such events, and I really must not take up any more of your time. I must return home."

"Please stay, Hope. I would like to talk to you more about your situation later. I have had my servants make up the guest room in my quarters for you. I will summon one of them to take you to your room and serve you as you see necessary. Anyway, I noticed that the back of your sweatshirt says you are a Goddess so you should be dressed like one!" He smiles, grinning from ear to ear.

"That is very kind of you Cornelius. How will I ever be able to repay you for your generosity?"

"Don't worry Hope, you don't have to repay me. It's my duty as emperor to provide my guests with anything they need. Now please, go and get ready. I think I might just be able to help you. If you want to, we can continue our conversation later."

"Thank you, Cornelius, I really appreciate everything you are doing for me but I don't think anyone can help me anymore."

"You are very welcome, Hope. Just don't lose your name!"

What does that mean? Then she smiles. "Oh yeah, Hope!"

But Hope is sceptical. Why is Cornelius wanting to help her? What is behind all of this? She still feels confused by everything that is happening to her and wishes she would wake up and find herself back in her bedroom... or does she? Her life is so deeply unhappy back in Edenton. This is all so strange and wonderful and scary at the same time.

There is a knock at the door. A woman comes in with beautiful gowns of silk across her arm. Hope chooses a long, purple gown with gold fringe and a gorgeous silk sash. Glittering jewels are laid out on an ornate dresser by another tall woman who has a face of deep seriousness about her. Hope has never had such expensive things. She hurries to have a shower and get dressed. She looks in the mirror. *I brush up well*, she smiles. *I look half decent*.

She is taken by a golden chariot to join Cornelius at the Colosseum as he had requested her to do so.

"Welcome to the Colosseum, Hope. This is where our gladiators do battle."

"I'm really sorry Cornelius but I don't fully understand how being here is going to help me in my life and the situation I currently find myself in."

"My aim here, Hope, is to show you that no matter what

the challenges you face the more you fight those challenges and succeed at them the stronger you will be in your own battle."

"So, are you saying I need to face this battle with those that took my children head on to be able to succeed?"

"Yes, that is exactly what I am saying, Hope. The gladiators that fight in this ancient arena were nothing more than slaves when they first came here but now they have grown stronger and stronger each time they fight. Even my best gladiators have to face the fight head on. It's a fight to the death. This is what I am saying to you. You need to face things head on to get what you want in life." Cornelius looks at Hope. "We all have things we are not proud of. Things we wish we could change. I speak from experience. But one thing I do know is that everyone is worthy of a second chance."

Hope really doesn't know what to make of Cornelius and continues to keep her guard up. She thinks to herself, "Cornelius seems a genuine guy who wants to help me but because of what has happened to me I really struggle to trust anyone that wants to help me. No one has ever genuinely wanted to help me before. Those who said they wanted to help actually didn't. They always took something from me."

Hope stays with Cornelius in the Colosseum and watches the gladiators fight but still can't see how this can help her. Hope wants to trust Cornelius but she has trusted many people in the past and has had that trust betrayed so finds it difficult to trust anyone anymore. How does she know that Cornelius is not going to do the same?

As the gladiators fight to the death in the Colosseum,

Hope turns to Cornelius and says, "I also don't think killing other people is going to help me in my life! Cornelius says "Hope, this is how things are here. I have the power to save a life and the power to end one. I was born into this role. I don't have a choice."

Hope retorts angrily, "Well then don't lecture me about turning my life around. I haven't had choice either. I didn't choose who to be born to. I didn't choose for the kindest, loveliest person to die. No one gave me a choice about being forsaken and abused or bullied." Her eyes flash with fury. Cornelius stares at Hope. He wants to tell her that she can still choose a better life but he realises that maybe he is being a hypocrite. Maybe he also needs to stop making excuses and change. Is that even possible? He remains silent contemplating this extraordinary woman.

They return to the palace where Cornelius asks his servants to take Hope back to her room to rest and freshen up. Before Hope retires to her room Cornelius asks Hope to join him later that evening for a meal. It appears that Cornelius seems to have a bit of a soft spot for Hope and wishes to get to know her more. Hope veers between wanting to go home, back to reality, but at the same time she wants to stay with Cornelius because she is beginning to get a sense of strength and maybe expectation when she is in his company.

Hope goes to her room where she sits by the window and looks out into the distance. All she can see is Roman temples and palaces and people moving around outside going about their day as normal. She wonders what life would be like for her living in the Roman empire but soon shakes that thought out of her mind. All she has on her mind for the first time in a long time is how to regain the care of her children.

She hears the sound of music wafting through the open window and shakes herself. She must prepare herself for the meal with Cornelius. Once ready she is taken down the marble stairway to the room she was in earlier with the massive table. Cornelius is already there, sat awaiting Hope's arrival. There are candles sparkling all around the room. Cornelius quickly rises to meet Hope as she enters the room. Cornelius invites her to join him at the table and points to a place setting next to his. He wants to talk to Hope whilst they enjoy their meal.

"How are you, Hope?" Asks Cornelius.

"I'm well, thank you for asking. I think I must be in a dream," replied Hope.

"You know, Hope, I want to thank you for what you said earlier. I haven't had the guts to change because this is how we do things here. Maybe you are right that I need to face up to my own fears. We both have to find the strength to change. We all have choices."

Hope looks at him with compassion. Cornelius reaches out and takes hold of her hand.

At his touch, Hope drops her fork with a loud bang. And then she is gone.

Chapter 3

Hope wakes with a start. There is a loud bang. Someone is bashing on her front door. She had taped up her letterbox – no more bills! No more bad news! "Get Lost!" she thinks and pulls the pillow over her head. She has just had some bizarre dream about the Roman Empire.

The pounding continues. She jumps up grabbing her dressing gown and hurries down the cluttered stairs. She is ready to punch whoever is out there. She squints and peers through the tiny hole to the scary world outside the door of her grubby flat. She can see him. A tiny little person stood looking back at her. He was staring straight into the lens as if he was reading her thoughts. Hope pulls away. Holding her breath, with her heart pounding in her chest, she is unable to move. Hope slowly ducks back to the hole and peers out again. He turns to leave. Her mind begins to race. *Open the door, Hope! You must open that door!*

"I can't!" She hears her own voice shouting in her ears. "HOPE! Open the door NOW!"

It seems like a lifetime passes but she grabs the door handle and yanks it open. She calls out, "Wait...I'm here."

The man in shorts is at the gate. Who wears shorts in February?! He looks kindly at her and sort of skips to the front door. He smiles at her but she avoids his gaze. Whether it is because she looks like a big kid in her dressing gown or her blond hair is in a fuzzy mess, she doesn't know but he seems to be chuckling. She remembers in some police evidence she was described as having dirty blonde hair. "Yeah, that's me," she thought, "I can't even do 'blonde.'"

The postman hands her a letter with one of those smiles that holds a secret. A secret that felt like he was on tiptoes of sharing. A plain, brown envelope is in his hand. He motions with a sweep of his hand, "This is for you," smiling all the while. Hesitantly, Hope reaches out and takes hold of it.

It is stamped 'Dorton County Council'. *Oh no! Why did she open the door?* In a trance she stares down at what has been delivered into her delicate fingers. Through clenched teeth she mutters "I hate them! I hate them." Some things just aren't bearable. She looks up but the postman has vanished.

She stares at the letter in her hands. She wants to ignore it, pretend it isn't there. She hadn't shared everything with Cornelius but he was the first person she had opened up to about her situation. Now, all the memories come flooding back. A gripping panic in her gut makes her want to vomit.

Going inside she leans against the wall trying to find something solid to hold her up. Tearing open the envelope she finds a letter.

She switches on the light in the hallway but the bulb has blown months ago. In the dim light she sees it is her once a year letter from her son's adopters. One day in three hundred and sixty-five she would find out about her boy. One whole year had to pass by. It is an anniversary she longs and waits for, yet dreads.

To write the year in the life of a child would require hundreds of books. Think of all a child would do and speak and learn and discover in one year! The first babbling words, the sleeping with their bum in the air, the mashed banana in their hair, the waving goodbye and clapping hands. The look of pure delight at a cat brushing up against the pushchair or the first ice cream and of course, the first tentative, wobbly steps.

But here is a single piece of A4 paper with writing on one side. She turns it over and there on the back was a child's drawing. A big dog on its back with a glowing yellow sunshine in the corner. She wants to cry and laugh. "What a clever boy. My son!"

Dear Hope
Archie is growing very big now. He loves playing
with balls and chatting about all things related to
tractors! We all went on a lovely holiday in the
summer. Archie rode on a pony. He said it was the

best part of our time away. He loves his nursery and has made lots of friends. The nursery say he is very bright and a real charmer. His favourite colour is purple. He painted this purple pony upside down because he said ponies like to be funny. He made sure the sun is shining brightly as he doesn't like rainy days. He is a happy little lad and everyone loves his cheeky grin. Wishing you well.

From

Sue and Alan

So, it's a pony not a dog! Of course it is. She folds the letter into her chest – his favourite colour is purple. He loves sunny days. "My boy, my little boy. I love the colour purple and sunshine and animals. He's a mini-me."

But then the questions begin tumbling around her head. "Did Archie paint that just for me? Does he know I am his REAL mummy? Could he even remember the times I spent at the children's centre where I rocked him in my arms and smiled at his beautiful face drinking in every single dimple and those lovely long eyelashes? Why have they put him in a nursery?" Hope would never have done that! If the court would have let her keep him, she would have been with him every single day. They probably work long hours and are never home.

Who was "We all had a lovely holiday?" Did they have lots of other children? He has lots of friends but does he even know he has a big brother and sister?

Archie has fair skin like her. Did they keep him out of the sun? Maybe they took him abroad. The thoughts that begin as a trickle whoosh around until they are spinning and swirling and flood her mind and she feels hot and sweaty. One thought now pervades her mind – "I need a drink!" She sinks down on the step. Her heart aches for just one hug. Maybe not even a hug, she could cope with a glimpse of him. She only has a recollection of him as a baby. But now he is far more than a toddler. He is a proper little boy.

If she could just see him and know he is happy that would be enough. But Hope knows that is a lie. If she saw Archie she would run and throw her arms around him, pick him up and kiss his chubby face a thousand million times and then run and run and run.

If only she could talk again to the man in her dream, Cornelius. It was rare that she had good dreams. Her way to get to sleep was either to get high or drunk. The tossing and turning at night and the haunting nightmares were more than she could bear. "If only it was real and I could escape to Rome." Her heart physically hurts. Hope drags her feet up the stairs, feeling lower than a snake's belly, but then her foot hovers over the step. Cornelius' words return to her mind. Holding her head up proudly she says out loud, "I opened the door!"

Chapter 4

'If the best moments in your life could be put in a jar, what would you put inside?' The article in the magazine left on the train seat led with that title.

Hope hadn't ever really thought about her 'best moments'. Most of her time is spent overthinking all of the bad decisions she has made, the way she has been lied about and mistreated, fear of the way ahead and the regret at the way her life has turned out. These thoughts would twist, turn, pull and ultimately exhaust her.

But today is going to be different. There is a reason to celebrate and this would be a 'best moment'! She is choosing not to lie in bed and wish the day away. Cornelius said everyone is worthy of second chances and she is going to try to live that. Today is her eldest son's eighth birthday! Eight years' ago today she held for the first time that rather big bundle – he was 9lbs 7oz! Something crazy and terrifying had happened on that day – Hope had become a "mummy"! Jay had finally made an appearance after being fourteen days overdue!

On all the birthdays after his forced removal from her care she would veer between crying and hating herself or begging God to let her see him or just getting absolutely smashed out of her face. Sometimes it was all three at once.

She hasn't seen Jay or her little girl, Madison since they

were placed in care. Initially she was 'allowed' two hours of contact every six weeks. Hope would often drink heavily the night before, trying to face the scab being pulled off the wound again. The goodbyes that keep repeating. She saw the look of hurt on her children's faces. They are growing and living but she has no part in that. Once a contact supervisor took her aside and said, "You shouldn't cry, you know. It's very upsetting for the children. Try to put their needs first." She stared at him trying to find words that wouldn't get her arrested.

Different supervisors turned up every six weeks to watch her interaction with her kids. Do animals in a zoo feel this sort of terror? Can anyone imagine the stress of playing with your children while someone else is writing notes about it?! Or how about when your child asks when they can come home? Try that for torture! If they are being naughty, should she tell them off? Will that look bad? Should she choose the game or should they choose the game? When she covered them in kisses does she look too needy, etc. Most mothers could never imagine the stress of playing with their children and being watched.

The joy at seeing them coupled with the pain that she knew it would end all too soon just added to the tension.

On the last occasion the staff told her that she smelled of drink and that contact couldn't go ahead. After that she stopped going. She couldn't cope. They were better off without her.

She had her 'goodbye contact' with her baby, Archie, two years ago. Their last contact was just an hour and a half together in a 'family' centre. Photos are taken and you try to embed your baby's face into every brain cell. His smile or the turning of his head, those little fingers and that soft downy hair. Each second passing was one less moment to draw him into her heart, to see him, to touch him. She took so many photos thinking this would preserve him and it did -as an infant. She left silently on that last day. She felt the handle of the door turn slowly in her hand like one who fears what will happen if the lock does indeed turn. The door opened and pain swept in with a force that almost killed her.

How do you say 'goodbye' to your own child? There is no 'good' about it. If a child died you could understand there is a parting that no one on earth can undo. But her children were living. They were somewhere in the world. Whenever she walked past a park or a school, she would scan the faces of the children just in case they were hers. But they never were.

Once when she was in town, she thought she saw Madison. Her heart skipped a beat. That hair, that funny little gait but then the little girl turned her head and the truth hit her hard. Frozen for a moment, no breath in her, she sat down at the back of a doorway. Tears slid silently down her drawn face. The darkness had regrouped and emptiness prevailed. No one noticed.

It was something most people could never understand or relate to. Although she had 'lost' her children there was little if no compassion. There was plenty of judgment. *Why didn't you leave your violent partner? Why did you choose him over your children? Why didn't you get help for your drinking? Your kids were hurt and you could have stopped that. You deserve it, you failed to protect them!* She had heard all of that and more. So if anyone asked her if she had kids she would lie. Lying about something so precious was traumatising. How can you lie about the best thing that ever happened to you? But telling the truth brought more questions and ultimately judgment. *Where are they? Couldn't you have fought harder? It's a shame you put your partner before your own kids. At least they are alive. Can't you just move on?*

She knows she deserves the scorn. What plays relentlessly in her head was worse. Hope runs herself down for everything. If she actually gets dressed, she tells herself, "Look at you! You look like a tramp". If she is undressed, "You are disgusting". If she smiles, "How can you smile? Your kids don't even live with you. You have no right to laugh." If she cried, "What a loser you are. No one loves you. You should cry! You are shit." This was her running commentary and it was hell.

But the last two weeks since she had had that crazy dream about Cornelius have made her start to think. Maybe she didn't have to accept the life she was living.

Her first accomplishment had been getting out of bed before one o'clock AND she brushed her hair! Next, a start to clear some of the rubbish off the floor of her flat. She wasn't sure where the floor was when she grabbed the carrier bag but now the carpet is actually visible. The number of bottles she collected was insane. "The evil grape! I must have killed off a lot of brain cells with that lot," she smirks. Another big success was she had actually gone to the laundrette and did a load of wash. She went late at night so no one was around. That evening she put sheets on her bed and felt proud. How lucky are people who don't overthink!

On the train she reads the article and looks out of the window. The train was carrying her towards Cromer, a seaside town which smelled of fish and chips and salty air. Today will be a good day.

Hope walks into town heading to the pier. She notices a young lad charging out from the amusement arcade with a Roman helmet and shield. She turns to the man nearby, "That helmet actually looks rather authentic but the shield is definitely wrong." The guy raises his eyebrows and stares at her oddly.

She walks on giggling to herself. Then she stops. Out of the corner of her eye she sees them and is frozen to the spot.

When Jay was born her Nanny had come all the way from Cornwall to the hospital. She came onto the ward in a flourish as only Nanny Jane could. She bellowed, "Where's my gorgeous granddaughter and the number one great grandson for the bestest Great Nanny there ever was?" People looked up but she didn't care. She spied Hope, gave a whoop and rushed over giving her the biggest hug! She had those types of arms that when they enclosed you, you were bigger than the world.

"Well, you did it, girl! Looking tenderly towards the baby lying on Hope's chest.

"And what a chubster he is! How are you feeling?"

"I'm kind of in shock. It hasn't really sunk in!"

"What's his name? Someone said you were naming him Elvis."

"No, I am not!" She laughed. His name is Jay – sort of after you, but don't tell Jimmy.

"Well, I brought you a ginger beer, two bags of sweeties

and some prawn cocktail crisps AND a pack of chocolate biscuits – all your favourites!"

"Jimmy didn't bring me anything. All he did say was he was glad it's not a girl!"

"He's a waste of space as I have told you a thousand times. But enough about him. For the little man I bought this!" She whipped out of her handbag the cutest, fluffy giraffe with a big blue ribbon tied around his neck. I have named him 'Eddie'. He will watch over our little fellow until we don't need to look after him no more."

Hope said, "Well, I think I need one too!

"You have got me for that, said Nanny Jane, pausing to gently pat the back of the little bundle on Hope's chest. "Know why I bought a giraffe?"

"No, but I reckon you are going to tell me," Hope chuckled.

"I wanted a peaceful animal. One that that don't prey on others. They are loyal but sensitive. I think they inspire us to stretch ourselves. More than what we think we can do." With that Nanny Jane stretched out her neck and pecked Hope with a big kiss on her forehead. Hope turned her face up and smiled at her nanny.

"Can I have a cuddle?"

"Of course! He's all yours."

Hope handed Jay to Nanny Jane who tenderly took him up in her arms and began to softly sing. It was an old song that Nanny Jane had sung to her a thousand times:

Held by nature
We are Surrounded by Love
Positive and kind
Always Held from Above

My dear little petal.
My sweet little pea.
Rocking in my arms like a little bumble bee.

Rainbows are out
The skies are all clear
I will always be here
To hold you near.

My dear little petal.
My sweet little pea.
Rocking in my arms like a little bumble bee.

So swaddle my baby
My baby I hold
A treasure more precious than
diamonds, rubies or gold.
(written by Tasha)

That happy moment. That joyful, beautiful moment has become a memory. Even memory has become a memory, she thought.

Chapter 5

Empty of all expression, Hope stands staring into the arcade. There in an enormous glass box must have been at least one hundred fluffy giraffes just like Eddie waiting to be won!

Hope searches frantically and finds a pound coin lurking at the bottom of her bag. After she hurriedly pushes it through the slot, the silver claws of the grabber jerks to life and begin to move. She clutches the knob in her hand guiding the grabber right over the head of a particular giraffe, one that seems to be looking at her. His head is poking out at the top of a mound of the others. She presses the button and the grabber begins to lower down right over 'her' giraffe. It grasps his head and begins to pull him out. The giraffe seemed to be slipping. He's slowly sliding forward when a single furry orange horn is caught dangling on the end of the claw.

Hope isn't breathing. She feels her hand become sweaty. She gently pulls the knob directly towards her. The grabber advances to the box where the giraffe could safely be dropped. At that moment she is filled with an immense exhilaration and shock. He is going to make it! He would be hers! She glances up momentarily. At the back of the glass box, she sees a mirror reflecting this moment back to her. The reflection is of a face captivated by pure joy. Her gaping eyes wide with surprise look back at her.

She blinks and blinks again. Where is she? What is this place? Why is she suddenly in a shop filled with cuddly toys?

Chapter 6

Year: 2023
Cat's Story

Bonnie, Calum Edith and Orion, have been sneaking into my bag lately to see what adventures they can get up to. While I am not looking, they are always on the lookout for more giraffes to rescue.

Now you must be wondering 'who are these characters and who am I?' This is where my story begins. I save giraffes. I had saved quite a few of them because there are a lot of giraffes out there who are lost and lonely that need rescuing.

Given the number of giraffes I have, I have had to work out each personality within the herd. Bonnie is a mother hen and likes to make sure they are all looked after. Calum acts like butter wouldn't melt in his mouth. Edith is very shy and, bless her, suffers from hard of hearing. They all have their own little personalities but one thing I do know is that they all love sausage rolls (so they are never safe if I bring them home from work) and they also love chocolate (hubby found out the hard way).

Edith, Rosemary, Orion and Phoenix eventually joined the family. At the beginning when I only had four giraffes I once caught them chattering to each other saying, "We only need to rescue another twenty-two giraffes then they will have the full alphabet of giraffes!" I told them an emphatic "No," as it's a tough job keeping this lot in check – not to mention making sure they are all fed with their favourite sausage rolls and chocolates.

However, Bonnie, Louise, Calum and Ian are very cheeky. One day they nicked my phone and rescued two more giraffes. They didn't stop there. They kept wanting to have another brother and sister to share their adventures with.

When I go to see my deaf friends, they absolutely love seeing my little giraffe family. Hearing what they have been up to is always amusing. They have either done something funny or are wearing something new. When my giraffes see their friends wearing something nice, they want my friend, Suzie, to make them something new so that they are not left out. It's a full time job looking after these 'raffs'.

Maybe you would like to know a little more about these cheeky characters?

Orion being the newbie to the family likes to get into a

lot of my things. He will jump into all of my zoom calls to say hello to everyone. He is quite nosey as he wants to know who I am talking to and who he can say hello to. He is very cheeky and loves to be at the centre of attention. Thankfully, my friends don't mind. They normally ask where the rest of the gang are and what are they doing so that they don't feel left out.

Orion adores being on the motorbike! He loves to see where I am going. However, the only thing he doesn't like is the rain. He gives me the silent treatment when it comes to the rain but that's something that I really can't help with. "I also hate the rain," I tell him, "But I have to travel in it to get to work." I have warned him that Britain isn't like other countries where we don't have the sun 24/7 as much as it would be nice. He soon dries off and has a snooze.

Edith has been learning a lot more sign language and her confidence has grown so much in the last few months. She is now going to be taking part in a performance, in front of a few friends, as she is wanting to get herself ready for the summer. When it's Bonnie's turn to perform at Deaf Feast, she is really happy that she is getting the chance to meet old friends and lots of new friends too. She can share her knowledge with all these new friends who all love that she is there to share her story and learn a new skill. When Edith is off with new people those deaf friends do miss her.

This past week I took the herd away to a few events. The first being a vintage car show. Calum was very happy at this as he loves looking around the cars. He is especially chuffed if he can get to sit in them as well! He was happy to snuggle up in my hoodie while I was looking around the cars. He then was wondering if he was going to be caught on camera as he could see lots of people with cameras. He is a bit of a poser is Calum!

He found the car museum so was looking around those cars in there and he really wanted to drive the racing car and shout "I am speedy!" but was cross that he couldn't see over the steering wheel. I then coaxed him out with a look around the other cars as I knew there were the cars that belonged to the royal family being stored there and was wondering if he was able to find them.

After about ten minutes Calum was able to find them. He got to look in a few of them and he was telling the people around the cars that he was a part of the royal family now. He then snuck into the car that once belonged to the Queen Mother even though he was told not to. What Calum didn't see was that there were police officers at the event.

As Calum got in the car, he was spotted by a copper so he was taken to the police car. They put poor Callum in the back seat and the police officer took a photo of him as he found it cute seeing this little giraffe's head poking out the barred window looking sorry for himself. He kept Calum there for about ten minutes before letting him go with the warning of not to touch anything like that again. Calum promised he wouldn't. The rest of the herd found it very funny as they could see the commotion and Calum's little sobs for help.

On Monday the herd got a special day out as we had driven from near Birmingham to Tamworth. We all got to eat a huge jacket potato from a famous food truck. Once the food had been eaten and a quick look around town, they all headed back to the motorhome to continue the journey off to Stonehenge. The little ones fell asleep as we made our way down the road. It was the first bit of peace all day!

When we arrived, we found out that they had closed the gates for that day so we parked up close by so that we could all jump out and get the photos when the last people had left as it would soon be sunset and the photos would look amazing to get Stonehenge with the sunset background.

When we reached the perfect spot, I lined them up to have the photo done but three of the Raffs all rushed off to be in the stone circle as to them it is a magical place and they were drawn to it. Calum on the other hand stayed seated for the photo and was taking in the view as to what was in front of him. Then all night I could hear "We are sleeping near the magical stones; we are sleeping near the magical stones" and "Why did they build it this way? Mummy, you must know the answer. You know everything."

I finally managed to get them to sleep on the promise that they could pay a visit to the visitors centre the following morning to learn why the stones were there, followed by the gift shop as long as they were on their best behaviour!

The following morning soon came around quick enough. I was woken by the sound of little hoofs jumping and their giraffe voices shouting, "Is it time to go and see the stones and the rest of Stonehenge yet?" I got everyone ready and packed up the van then drove down the visitor's centre so that we could pay to get in and look around.

The Raffs were on their best behaviour the whole time we were there so I told them they could go and pick one thing each from the gift shop. I was running around dealing with Calum, the little rascal as he wanted to touch everything in the shop!

Bonnie, who is rather cautious, then whispered to me, "There's a lady who has been watching us. She's been watching us all for a little while now and hasn't taken her eyes off Edith. I am worried about what she might do."

I turned to where Bonnie was pointing with her hoof at a woman standing by the cuddly toys. She was definitely talking to herself. "Is this woman okay?" I thought.

She was mumbling "Not again! Damn that mirror!" She looks around confused "Why here?"

I decided to approach this strange woman. She looked frantic and confused. I wondered if she is ok or needs help. What is this about a mirror? I was hesitant at the beginning because I didn't know whether she needs help or not. I care a lot about others because of who I am and how the giraffes have opened my eyes to the possibilities of a different world where everyone cares for each other.

As I walked up to her, the woman looked wary of me, but then the Raffs suddenly poked their heads out over my shoulders, and they were all giggling. The woman was shocked but intrigued. She said, "I was just trying to win one of these! Am I going mad, but did I hear them speaking?" I introduced myself to her and she tells me her name is Hope.

I shared with Hope the story of my Raffs and how I discovered there were many giraffes to be rescued. I thought maybe I could do my bit. Their stories broke my heart. It made me so sad to hear of how they felt unwanted but it gave me comfort in my own sadness. I added "I guess we can all find a way forward even when there is pain in our hearts."

I never dreamed one day I would one day have twelve to look after!! At that point Edith, the raff who has hearing loss, signs, "I love you!" They all copied, and Sydney gave me a cheeky kiss on the cheek. We all started to laugh.

Seeing how caring I am with the raffs, Hope asked me, "Do you have children?"

It was my turn to be wary and hesitant. I don't share my story with just everybody. I took a deep breath... I could sense that this woman has a lot of pain. Something has gone terribly wrong for her. However, I was scared I would be judged because that's how I always feel. I explained about my beautiful, gorgeous children – all four of them. Hope is broken by what I am telling her. She is in tears.

Bonnie, (my mother hen raff), jumps into my arms and cuddles me because she can see that I have shared something so personal and precious. The others put their arms around me.

In that moment Hope starts to explain her story. She lets me know that she is grateful to have met me, as today is such an important day for her.

She would have loved to have shared the journey today with her children. They had been taken from her. She was in the arcade trying to win a giraffe. It brought back memories of her eldest son's little giraffe he had as a baby.

"When he was born it was the perfect moment in my life."

He was given a cuddly giraffe by her late grandmother. It was his special giraffe which went everywhere with him. His giraffe was called Eddie. When they took her child away Eddie went as well. Every time she saw a giraffe it would remind her of happier times. She hoped her son still had Eddie.

Hope explained she had been wandering past the amusement arcade and saw the giraffes in the grabber machine. She desperately wanted to win one. At home in a special box, she had a little outfit that all of her babies had worn. She wanted to win the giraffe and put the outfit on the little giraffe. If the courts hadn't been so quick to believe the lies from her ex and children services she would not be in this position.

By this time, we had managed to walk all the way round the stones and had headed back towards the gift shop. I had spoken to Hope about a few places that had supported me and if she wanted to, she could take their details so that she didn't have to feel so alone. "It's important to get support. Don't carry all this pain alone."

Hope explained to me that since losing her children a lot of her friends had stopped talking to her and she felt like she has no one who understands how she feels. "Being so alone now is beyond terrible". This is something I know to a tee, so I passed over the details and I hoped that she felt in some small way she wasn't alone anymore.

Hope looked up with tears in her eyes. All of the sudden Edith, a very special raff, jumped into Hope's arms and gave her a kiss on the cheek. At that moment, they all looked around but Hope had disappeared.

Chapter 7

Riding on the bus always makes Hope feel horrendously anxious. She feels people are looking at her. Someone on that bus might know about her kids. Maybe a mum from the school would be on the bus. What if she sees Jimmy or he actually gets on this bus? She starts scanning the faces of the passengers. Did she hear the young woman at the front of the bus whisper something to the girl sat next to her as she walked down the aisle? At every stop she feels panic that Jimmy or one of his family will get on the bus.

Hope slumps down low into her seat leaning her head against the window, her cheek wet by the pane of glass. She will be getting off at the stop near the hospital. She tries to focus on the world outside the bus. *Breathe, Hope, Breathe.* Only three more stops and she would get off to attend a social services meeting. They called it LAC review which means a 'looked after child' review. Her anxiety is now through the roof.

The bus pulls up at the stop and Hope hurries off with her hood pulled up over her head. She takes a deep breath relieved to get out into the open air despite the cold air biting at her face. She looks over at the hospital. At the sight of the grey brick building, she remembers Archie's birth and the memories all come flooding back. The nightmare of losing her children didn't start then. It started well before Archie was born.

Chapter 8

At the beginning the Police didn't have serious concerns for the safety of her children. Over time, however, the calls to the police became more frequent. One neighbour was becoming more concerned for the children or maybe she just liked the drama. Police cars turning up outside, knocks at the door, "No officer, everything is ok. Sure, you can come in." Net curtains twitch.

She ignored the letter social services posted through her door. The police advised her to contact Women's Aid but she didn't feel she needed help. Jimmy was the one who needed help. He had turned to even harder drinking after losing his dad to cancer. He didn't know how to cope with the loss so he and the bottle became even better acquainted.

Yes, she liked a drink but she could stop when she wanted. And she could. She could go for weeks, sometimes even months without a drink but if she started she would finish. She couldn't just have 'a drink'. It was all or nothing.

Drinking had been the norm throughout her childhood. When she was around eleven years old, her mum would send her to the shops to steal it. She knew better than to argue. Taking along her backpack she would throw in a few tins of spaghetti hoops, some strong lager, a loaf of white bread, marg and maybe a can of cola. Somehow the cans of lager never made their way onto the supermarket conveyor belt. She quickly learned to show no emotion as she chatted to the checkout cashier while the cage of her lungs was pounding. The straps of the backpack would slip over her small shoulders and out onto the street she strode. How do you feel really pleased with yourself when you are a thief? Because you know your mum is going to be a lot happier when you return. She might even say something good about you and you won't have to deal with a mother who desperately needs a drink.

Chapter 9

One night when Jimmy got home from work he started drinking heavily. Hope could tell things weren't going to end well. The mood in the house was tense and he was starting to bellow out abuse at her. Ignoring him, she got the children ready for bed. She was heading towards the bathroom when she turned away from him. He grabbed hold of her by the hair. He flipped her around and was screaming in her face. Hope didn't move. Like the rat finally cornered by the python, she knows to be still. The monster has made his appearance. He towered above her, eyes crazed and empty of expression. Then those thick rope-like hands grabbed hold of her neck. The claws began to squeeze and constrict around her throat. The power of a thousand warriors crushes out her breath. She knew this time he wasn't going to stop. Within seconds her arms dangled out alongside her body as her lungs had all but given up for a sliver of air. Staring into his bloodshot eyes there is one thought, "He's going to kill me."

A delicate figure squeezed between her legs and those of her attacker. Jay was only six years old. His small hands strain, reaching up, to grab hold of his father's elbows. Such a small child trying his best to protect his mother.

Jimmy grabbed hold of Jay's arm and snapped him up in the air, his body dangling momentarily before he threw him like a rag doll across the hallway. Jay hit the wall with a thud. The force of his little body against the wall caused the mirror above his head to be jolted. It shuddered and toppled off its hook.

Hope could see it all happening. Everything slowed down. She saw the mirror land with a force that knocked the child to the floor. He screamed as he hit the floor. The mirror smashed against the grey, bare tiles. A large piece of glass ricocheted off the tiles and pierced the side of Jay's cheek. A cloudburst of shattered glass sparkled across the hallway covering everything. Blood began to pour out from the child's head onto the gleaming glass. Maddie was only two and a half years old. Her tiny bare feet began to run. Hope hadn't even realised she was there.

The child's soft, perfect feet were being shredded by the shards of sharp glass. The torment of her screams echoed down the hallway. A horror film couldn't have been worse. The fear and alarm was reflected through the jagged pieces of mirror lying all around the floor.

What happened next is what she couldn't forgive herself for. Jimmy stormed out of the house and she was left to try to help the children. She cleaned up their cuts and then put them to bed. They were whimpering in their sleep. She decided the next day to keep them off school. She didn't take them to the doctor. She was afraid of what they might say and that they would contact social services. Jimmy returned the following morning. He looked subdued and mumbled he was sorry but he was 'struggling with the death of his father'. Hope was so angry but also afraid. She knew better than to say a word.

She took the children to school the following day. She had bruising all around her neck but wore a scarf to hide it. The shame was intense.

Jay had PE at school the next day. When he took off his t-shirt to get changed his teacher saw the terrible purple bruise on his shoulder. Her mouth fell open and gasped as she looked at the injury to this little boy. She asked him how it happened and he went really quiet. She had noticed the plaster on his face and asked if everything was ok. He told her he was worried about his mummy because his daddy hurts her. The whole story came out.

The school immediately contacted social services. They took Madison out of her nursery class. They checked her over and discovered the cuts on her feet. Emergency action was taken to remove the children. They were aware of the police call outs and the accident in the car and that Hope had never responded to their letter or answered the door when they came to speak with her.

Hope asked Jimmy to leave. She told him the relationship was over and she could no longer stay with a man who was violent. She knew she deserved better but he didn't go straight away. He cried and begged her to give him another chance. He told her they needed each other to get the kids back. She was torn. It was crazy. How could she love a man like that? She had even lied during the court hearing to say that she was driving their car after it had ploughed into a ditch. This was to 'protect' Jimmy because he had been off his face that night drinking. She never stopped to consider that he hadn't protected her.

There was always an excuse as to why he would hurt her and fail her. But after eight years you get used to being treated this way. You start to believe that you are no good and that you don't deserve any better. Hope learned too late that you can love someone and them not be good for you.

Hope wiped her nose on her sleeve. She had also felt terrified about being on her own. No money and no friends. Her life had been one of hurt and pain and now she didn't have her children. People talk about 'choices.' Where were her choices?

Social Services didn't believe she had ended the relationship. They said she had failed to protect the children. She can now see parts of what they were saying but they twisted so much of what she told them. How could she trust social services? They hadn't protected her when she was little.

And where in the social worker's statement were the very good things she had done and been? People would say, "Yeah well that's not what they are there to do – to talk about your good points. If you are in court, they are there to provide evidence that you aren't a 'good enough parent.'"

Of course, the foster carers fell in love with her children. Who wouldn't? The court decided they should stay in long term foster care until they were eighteen. And Hope's world crashed into a million pieces.

Chapter 10

Meeting a 'normal' guy had been something new to Hope. She had met Richard online at this lowest point in her life. The children were gone. Jimmy had been cheating on her and his drinking was out of control. She eventually went to a women's refuge after one terrible beating but it was all too late. She knew then she ought to have left him years before. The regret resurfaced daily. Her loneliness at his departure was only eased by the relief to not be walking on egg shells all the time. But there were days when she wanted him back. It was all she had ever known.

Hope found it hard to make friends. Being shy and scared of the world doesn't help when you actually want people in your life. Drinking helped ease the anxiety but the next day it would all come flooding back. It was a relentless cycle. Like those magic candles you blow out on a cake, making a wish, but they flicker straight back to life. She would puff out the myriad thoughts that plagued her by numbing herself with alcohol or drugs only to find they were resurrected the next morning and joined by others! It was exhausting.

So she used her phone to live her life; scrolling her life away and drinking to forget. She would go on dating apps. It was fun being chatted up by strangers. She sent a cute guy a message.

"Hi, I like your mug." His photo was him posing holding

a mug that said "chaos coordinator."

He wrote back. "Your mug isn't too bad either," which made her laugh. His photo was of a man with deep blue eyes and sophisticated grey hair. He was handsome and funny.

They started texting every day. One night he wrote "We should meet." Her heart skipped a beat. She knew he was too good to be true but she had fallen head over heels in love.

He spoiled her. Showed her tenderness and a kindness that she was desperate for. When he held her in his arms she felt safe and protected. His name was Richard and she felt she had won the lottery!

She told him everything - All about the court, her children, her whole sad life. He encouraged her to fight to get the kids back. He said she shouldn't give up and to appeal. When she explained it was all too late and they would never give the kids back. His response was adamant, "Of course, you should get your kids back! You are their mother and if it hadn't been for Jimmy they would still be with you. I will do anything I can to help you." And the first thing he did was help her to reduce the vodka. Sure, they enjoyed drinking together but now it was just drinks and fun. She didn't need the vodka when Richard was around. She didn't mind him drinking. It wasn't like Jimmy. He wasn't an angry drunk. He was a soppy drunk.

True to form he was lying asleep on her couch one night when the phone lit up. He normally switched his phone off when they were together. "Our time is our time. I don't want any interruptions when I am with you." She melted into him. "How could a man love her like this?" she wondered. It was so rare when they could meet because he was constantly travelling. His work involved tech, crypto and something else she didn't understand. The glow of the phone caught her eye. She leaned over and read. "Hi Honey, what time are you getting home tomorrow? I miss you. Hope the meeting is going well. Wifelet x."

He had a wife!

"How could you! I trusted you, you lying bastard." They had a blazing row, her new life deleted by a text.

Crying and begging, Richard confided in Hope that his wife Vicky was controlling and their marriage was desperately unhappy. Richard wanted to leave Vicky but he just didn't know how.

"I was scared if I told you about her, you would end what we have. You have given me the love I have been searching for all of my life." He sobbed as he told her about his regrets at not leaving Vicky. He kept crying "I can't live without you. Please don't end this."

She was devastated to learn that he was married but bizarrely felt sorry for him. She knew what it was like to feel trapped. She realised that he needed her as much as she needed him. After the screaming and crying, Richard lay in her arms and she decided she would help him to be free. They made love again and again that night. He had to be hers. It just had to be. She pushed away the thoughts that there might be a loving wife waiting at home for him.

They made plans how they would be together. He was going to see a solicitor. Their love wasn't going to be destroyed by that woman. From now on Hope and Richard referred to his wife as SV – "Sick Vic."

When Richard wasn't around, vodka made a return. She could only think of him being with 'her'. Hope began drinking to stave off the anxiety. She couldn't cope without him. They argued more as her mood became increasingly insecure and her overthinking was out of control. Then the vomiting began. She knew that queasy feeling. Her periods had always been irregular but the two little blue lines told her what she already suspected.

Richard received the text "I need to see you. It's an emergency." He came as soon as he could. When Richard rushed through the door Hope began crying.

"I can't stop long. Is it to do with the kids? Are they alright?"

"It's to do with kids" she paused hesitatingly, "but not mine." She then turned her face towards Richard. "Ours."

There was a heavy silence. Richard's face changed. First, it was shock then it was a hardness that she recognised, the twisting of his mouth.

"Are you pregnant?"

Hope nodded. She looked into his eyes searching for reassurance.

"Hope, you need to get rid of it. We aren't ready for a baby. This isn't the time. I'm still trying to work things out for us."

"But now you can tell SV about us! If she knows you are having a baby with someone else, she will one hundred percent let you go!"

"Don't call her SV," he snapped. Her name is Vicky."

Like a bucket of ice water thrown over her, her heart must have stopped momentarily. There is a suffocating silence then Hope exploded.

"What the hell? Are you serious? When did you all the sudden get protective over her?" Hope screamed.

"Hope, you don't understand. It's not that simple," he murmured reaching out, trying to draw her close to him. This charm offensive wasn't going to work. Hope had no intention of backing down. If Richard loved her as he told her he did a thousand times or more then he would understand why. They could have the life they both longed for. She could start over. Hope ripped her arms away from him.

"I am not having a termination! You need to know that is the last thing I am going to do. Having an abortion at seventeen was hard enough. I don't want to go through that again. We can have this baby together or I will have it alone."

"Hope, you aren't being reasonable. Come on, you just had your kids taken off you. Social Services will be all over you in a heartbeat. You aren't in an emotionally stable place to look after a child and you know it."

"I know you didn't just say that!" Hope barked. "I am as stable as the next woman. You have made me a wreck by all the secrecy and the lies and not leaving SV!" She shouted making particular emphasis of those two letters.

"Hope, think of all the drinking you have done. What effect would that have on a baby? You can't even cope a day without it." The row became louder and fiercer.

The pressure was building in the room. A furious,

boiling rage tipped her over the edge. Waves of anger exploded and Hope started punching Richard. He got hold of her and was shouting at her to calm down. She was screaming and kicking him simultaneously. She pulled away in fury. He was trying to grab her arms to stop her landing blows on him. He shoved her and Hope fell to the ground. He looked at her then turned, throwing his fist into the door. A big hole appeared but not as big as the one inside her heart.

"You are the same as Jimmy! There is no difference between the two of you. Only you beat me emotionally as well." There was a loud knock at the door. Everything stopped. Richard walked over and slowly opened the door. Someone had called the police. Hope ran to them and said, "Take this man away. He is beating me and is an abuser."

That was the last time she saw Richard but she knew she was going to be seeing him very soon – once this baby was born. And she would tell the court everything. She would tell him what a liar and cheat and manipulator he is! They would never give her baby to Richard and Vic.

But, of course, that is what the court did.

Chapter 11

She looks up at the hospital and remembers going through the doors of the 2nd floor of the maternity ward.

"I think I am in labour," Hope said breathlessly. Her labour pains had started and her waters had broken. Just walking from the taxi to the maternity unit had caused her to be out of breath.

"Well, you're in the right place," said the midwife. "Let me bring up your records. What's your name, dear?"

Hope waited while the midwife tapped the characters of her name into the keyboard. Was it her imagination or did she see the midwife's eyes flicker momentarily as she looked at the screen?

"I'm just going to get your file. Take a seat.'

The midwife returned and placed the file on the desk and starts typing into the computer. Hope's name was in bold capitals on the front of the file. The file seemed rather large. What was written on those pages? Did they know about her being raped at the age of seventeen? Were the details there of her loss of Jay and Maddie and that she had failed to protect them? Did they know she had tried to take her life after the rape?

Hope sat down wearily in the chair. The pains were beginning to grow. There was a couple sitting nearby holding hands. The woman looked like she was going to pop. Her partner began stroking her back and brushed away the stray strands of hair that had fallen around her face. He put his head next to hers and was speaking softly to her.

"I am all alone in this," thought Hope. She felt a pang of deep sadness. "People don't know what they have got."

The midwife stood up and went to speak to a colleague. Hope heard the dreaded words 'social worker' and then the other nurse turned her head away from the other woman and looked at her. Hope lowered her head and turned towards the wall.

She tried to focus on the posters on the wall. Heaving herself out of the chair she followed the woman from the desk. She had now taken on an authoritative tone, "You will need to stay on the ward once we book you in. When the baby is born you will not be allowed to leave until social services arrive." She paused and said, "Well, of course, you are free to leave", she said, "but not with the baby."

Social Services had carried out assessments of her during her pregnancy. Given the recent removal of Jay and Maddie, her emotional outbursts, the incident when she was drunk and went to Richard and Vicky's house with a pocket knife in her bag and her background, they considered that the baby should be placed in interim care upon its birth. Further assessments would be carried out after her baby's birth.

They explained that their plan was to remove the baby from the hospital once he was born. In order to do that they would have to apply to the court to get a judge to agree to make an interim care order. This hearing would take place the day after this little one would come into the world.

The other midwife approached her. She smiled at Hope with a look of pity on her face and asked how she was feeling. Hope felt tears welling up. She blinked repeatedly to try and stop the signs of her distress becoming a flow of tears. How was she feeling? When anyone showed her kindness, it made her want to cry. Holding in the pain was essential. She was scared if she started to cry, she wouldn't be able to stop. They're going to take this baby out of me and then they're going to take it from my life, Hope thought trembling. She whispered, "I can't do this." The midwife put her hand on her arm. "You are going to be just fine," she said kindly.

Hope wondered if maybe this is simply a nightmare. *I will just wake up and realise it was nothing at all, thank God*. But throughout her whole life she had been wanting to wake up. The reality was she was wide awake. It was no dream.

She had always wanted to be a mum. Her childhood was a memory of rejection and neglect. She hadn't been brought up; she had been dragged up. Being a better parent than what she had experienced as a child wasn't going to be much of a challenge is what she had thought. Little had she known.

The last she had heard, her father was at His Majesty's pleasure. Her mother had struggled with drink and domestic abuse for as long as Hope could remember. If it wasn't her dad, it was some new man coming into the house. Her memories included a lot of shouting, pushing, crying, screaming and then the dreaded silence as she hid under the bed. Her mother walking out of her life is a faded memory. It was only her Nanny Jane who had tried her best to protect Hope but she had lived on the other side of the country in a small flat and her husband had been an invalid.

The Doctor pulled back the curtain of her cubicle with real authority. It reminded Hope of a magician sweeping back the curtain to display the woman cut in two. The doctor begins to explain the procedure. Hope was trying to pay attention but it was all a haze.

Like the times spent with social workers carrying out her pre-birth assessment, the words would float over her head, swirl around the room and then seep out through the cracks in the small windows. Some words would land in her mind with a thud – Abuse, trauma, significant harm, adoption.

The prebirth assessment involved meeting with a social worker over several weeks to determine whether Hope could provide what they called 'good enough' care for her baby. They asked lots of questions and typed into their laptop copious notes but they were never checked by the person giving the information to ensure they are accurate. She realised later just how important that would be. They never once asked her what she would like to be written down.

What exactly did they want from her? What were the 'right' answers? If she showed too much emotion, would she be deemed unstable. If she appeared stoic, would she be deemed hard and unfeeling. She accepts that many times she would drink before she went to these meetings to steady her nerves. One of the social workers asked her if she had been drinking and she said she hadn't. She knew she hadn't believed her. And she was right. It was in the report.

One particular question that stood out to her as unbelievably stupid was "Did you understand that turning up at Richard and Vicky's house with a knife in your bag was serious?" Do social workers live in the real world? Heck yes, she knew it was serious!

The day after the birth there was an interim court hearing. It was decided that her baby would be best placed with Richard and Vicky. Hope was considered a risk of significant physical and emotional harm to her children.

Hope didn't go to the court hearing. Her solicitor said she would cover everything. She would explain how Hope was committed to caring for Archie and had made a great deal of changes.

Hope also didn't go because she knew that the powerful always win. Social services were the 'professionals'. They had compiled a history and a 'chronology' of all the pain, trauma and heartache that she had experienced in her life. It read like a charge sheet. How was she to blame for so much of what was written there? She hadn't chosen her childhood. For sure, she had made some bad choices but they didn't bother to write any of the good things she ever did in her life.

Richard and Vicky had a beautiful home, good jobs and knew how to impress. She stayed in the hospital while the court hearing was taking place, holding Archie and kissing his face and whispering how much she loved him. She told him she would fight for him and no matter what happened she would always love him. Hope looked around the ward and could see all the other mothers cradling their babies or changing their nappies. Life would go on normally for them. They would gather up their things and someone would be there to help them carry the many cards and presents or even flowers that they had been given and they would walk out of that hospital feeling excited and exhausted but relieved. They would start their new beginning.

Her mobile rang. She picked it up quickly. "Please God." It was her solicitor. "Hope," there was a pause. "I am sorry but the court has made the Order."

Hope doesn't remember anything else that was said. She would walk out of that hospital, her heart breaking and alone. She waited until the social worker came. The young woman who could not have been more than twenty-two years old didn't look her in the eye. She mumbled something about contact as she lifted her Archie out of the cot.

Hope had planned on clutching Archie to her chest and making the social worker try to prise her baby from her but she couldn't do it in the end. She stood by the little, clear plastic cot looking into the empty place where her son had been fast asleep. Out of the window she saw the social worker put her baby in a car seat and drive away. Across the ward a slim, petite young woman with long, dark brown hair was looking at her. Hope saw a tear running down the woman's face. She turned away and left.

Exiting the hospital with a carrier bag of her things and a few baby-grows she wanted to die. She waited at the bus stop wishing she could throw herself in front of it but she was too depressed. Her hormones were everywhere. Her milk was coming in. She was returning to her flat where the Moses basket and the baby bath and all the things she had bought for her little one waited for her and her child.

Social had told her she needed to show she was prepared for her baby and she had done what they asked. She had spent every penny and more on buying the baby the things he would need to be cared for by her, his mummy. How was she going to go home with empty arms? How could she look at those things which required a baby? *I can't go home but I have nowhere else to go.*

She remembers the words of that midwife as she was packing up her bag, "Now, love, don't go and get yourself pregnant again. That won't do you any good, you know. There are ways to stop that." Hope gave a weak smile but her heart was utterly shattered.

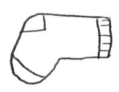

Sometimes the pain comes out of nowhere. Once she was looking for her keys and, in the search, found a little white sock behind a cupboard. Her sobs would have probably been heard by the neighbours in the flat next door. Staring at the small sock she sank to her knees and cried until there was nothing left, her tears wetting the tiny remnant of her son and what had never been. She went immediately to the kitchen and got out a bottle.

But there was one occasion of humanity that made a difference. She had gone to the contact centre to see Archie. The person supervising her contact sat in a chair opposite her with his notepad on his lap and his pen poised. He looked bored.

Being a newborn, Archie never stirred. He slept the entire time. What could the supervisor write if Hope did absolutely nothing for one hour? Hope just sat there, passively, Archie lying in the crook of her arm. She didn't speak. she had nothing to offer. Even her eyes felt numb. Looking at him she could sense her child drifting further and further from her as irreversible rift was forming. Like the two tectonic plates moving away from one other causing the African rift, a large divide was already there.

The hour ended and Archie was put in his car seat and taken out by a stranger. Leaving the centre, she made eye contact with no one and said nothing. Anger, hurt and despair hardened within her.

There was a tree and a square of grass at the corner of the building. Hope slumped down under the tree. Her arms were around her knees and her head rested on them. She looked off into the distance. The contact supervisor walked past her to his car. She only was aware of him returning when he stood over her. Looking up, Hope stared at him coldly. Then something so unexpected happened. He knelt down next to her and said quietly, "Are you ok?" Those three simple words touched her and she began to cry.

All these haunting memories of years ago were flooding back. She looks down at the puddle at her feet. She saw the saddest re-flection in the water. A bus whooshes past spraying water everywhere. She blinks and then blinks again...

Chapter 12

Year: 1970
Tracey's Story

Sophie's life had been what she thought of as idyllic and everyone always commented on how lovely her family was and how much of a team they were. She had been such a positive person who always had a smile on her face. She would find time for others and help in any way she could. She hated to see anyone struggle.

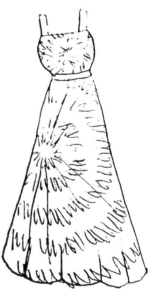

She was always listening to music on the radio and loved to sing along with David Bowie as she danced around the kitchen.

She was very much a hippie in her tie-dyed maxi dress. She loved expressing herself through her clothes. People always noticed her.

Rachael was a parent at her children's school. A woman in her forties, she dressed smartly with her long hair always tied up tightly in a bun. She wasn't like Sophie, with her messy tousled hair and her very hippy style, bright colours and often mismatching outfits.

Sophie thought she knew Rachael really well. She often went to her house for a cup of tea and a chat. Rachael often offered advice as she had two adult children. Sophie felt she trusted her and that she would always be there for her in any way she could.

Other mums told Sophie that Rachael was not all she made herself out to be and was not honest. Some even referred to her as a trouble maker but Sophie did not like to listen to the playground gossip preferring to make her own decisions. Sophie did as she always had – she saw the best in Rachael. Anyway, Rachael had confided in her so much about struggles she had faced in her childhood and troubles she had faced as a parent to a disabled child. However, Sophie would soon realise that Rachael was to be part of a catalyst of the destruction of Sophie's family and whole world and very nearly her life.

Sophie had taken some of her children out for a day and they all had lots of fun, looking at flowers, climbing trees and rolling down a grassy bank. On Sophie's return home her partner and other children told her about Rachael wanting to see her. They said she had been round to the house on numerous occasions.

Sophie didn't think much about it as she was tired and achy from her busy day and all she wanted to do was rest on her bed for an hour or so and rest her tired legs before cooking the children's tea and then of course the rush of bedtimes. Sophie had only been on her bed for ten minutes when there was a loud knock at the door.

Her partner called up to her that it was Rachael. Even

though she called down to ask her if she could speak with her tomorrow as Sophie was so tired, Rachael said 'No.' So Sophie, not wanting to disappoint anyone, went to speak to her. Rachael insisted on coming in and began telling Sophie that she had been doing too much. Despite Sophie telling her how tired she was it fell on deaf ears. Rachael's behaviour became very erratic and out of character but Sophie kept quiet as she just wanted her to leave. Sophie did not like confrontation.

This was the worst mistake she could have made and she should not have ignored the warning signs but again naivety took over from the red flag that what was glaring her in the face.

All through her time in Sophie's house, Rachael was talking *at* her rather than *to* her and she started to feel very anxious about the way and the context of Rachael's conversation. She was taking over Sophie's home telling her things that she did not like about Sophie's home and her parenting and even more was being very bossy. Sophie was totally overwhelmed by Rachael's behaviour and internally was hoping she would hurry up and leave.

The next day Rachael did to Sophie what she had previously done to others and what Sophie had been warned about so many times – she made false allegations that Sophie was hurting her children and had mental health issues to both the police and social welfare officers.

This was to have devastating results and like a tornado, normal life was taken away. This was to have horrendous results for Sophie's children and her.

In her naivety Sophie thought that the truth would be seen as she knew there would be records for Rachael having done this before to other families and having had a very bad problem with cannabis and shoplifting offences going as far as to have had the police attending and resulting in her being arrested on numerous times but how wrong she was. None of this was seen and as much as she told them and showed them evidence, they all seemed to be uninterested.

Her new nightmare took her to lows which she could never have imagined she would be in. She had heard of others but never imagined it would happen to her. She spent every day in her bedroom closed off from her emotions. She shut out everyone, not sure who to trust. She believed that doing this was in the best interests of her children. She really couldn't see a way out of this and would wake each day hoping it was just a bad dream but, no, it was her reality.

She fought hard to stay in the family home thinking she was protecting her children but she was actually destroying herself. In fact, her children were seeing her crumble. Sophie did not realise that her children were picking up on just how low she had become; she thought that she was hiding it from them. That made her hate herself even more as she had always strived to be the best mum that she could be but now she was, in her mind, failing everyone. Sophie thought about ending her life as she could not think of any other way to escape the pain.

Sophie reached out to her doctor as she had been the one person who had offered her any support and always listened. It was the one place she felt heard. On the day that she went to see her doctor as she sat in the waiting room, she opened another letter that she had picked up from the door mat on her way out of the house. It was yet another letter from the social welfare officer that was full of negativity about her and her parenting that she knew was not true and if only they had listened to her.

On entering the doctor's room and seeing the doctor's kind, caring, friendly face asking those words "How are you?" Sophie broke down and putting her head in her hands crying said the words that will echo in her memory forever "Can I have some antidepressants to numb me out of my life please?" She just wanted this nightmare over.

This was an all-time low pathway that she had never envisaged her life being so bleak. From this point Sophie attended meeting after meeting with Social Welfare always hoping that each would be the one where she was finally heard. But with every glimmer of hope it was extinguished as soon as it was ignited. Sophie exhausted herself mentally making phone calls to always face dead ends in the maze that was her life.

Finally, she was given details of a group for any woman to have a cup of tea and get support from each other. She was very apprehensive about joining the group but instead of facing yet more disappointment she was met with friendly smiles from the other ladies who she found had equally faced injustice and had their own stories. The problem was Sophie didn't know who to trust. Even her own family stopped all contact despite knowing how low she was.

Her stepfather and then her close friend had taken their own lives due to mental health struggles. She had listened to her mum say, "If only he had said something to me" when talking about her stepfather's passing. Yet when

Sophie, her own daughter, had reached out to her, her response was "This is your problem. You brought this on yourself."

For Sophie this felt so unjust as when she was in her twenties her mother had relied on her to give support because her mum suffered with insomnia and severe anxiety. Her mum would come to Sophie's place and Sophie would cook for her to make sure she ate. She also did her shopping for her and helped in any way she could even though she was so young herself.

This all felt very unjust. Sophie found herself relying on strangers for help which felt wrong but not all these people were good for her. Sophie was usually the one helping and offering support, now she was relying on others. She felt like she was in a big deep hole and as fast as her fingers reached to the top someone would come and stamp on them and she was right back down again.

The lovely doctor made referrals for her. One referral was to a psychotherapist who Sophie connected with straight away. She talked Sophie through the things going on for her and helped her to see them in another light. This had previously not been a thing she could do as Sophie was used to helping others but not herself.

She was also not used to hearing kind words said about herself. This would make her cry as she had been hating herself for what she saw as being a failure to her children.

Sophie was set goals and for the first time in a long while she saw things in another perspective and dug her heels in to take on the fight with a new found calmness. This therapist had set her a goal of attending a professionals meeting and keeping control of her emotions. Sophie decided that she was ready to take this on and set off to the meeting with all of the metaphorical tools ready in her head. She was going to keep her feet on the ground and take deep breaths. She was going to look at the social welfare officer and imagine he was her grandfather, a man who had always been a support to her but had now passed away. She imagined he was standing behind the social welfare officer and this gave her a focus.

At the next meeting she did not cry or let her emotions take over! She was elated and left the meeting feeling ecstatic. She went off to the shops to treat herself as a way of a reward. As she got to the counter clutching the chocolate treat she had chosen she realised that she had left her handbag in the meeting room. She had been so happy she had completely forgotten to pick up her bag. So she had to go back to the meeting room to retrieve her bag.

She got on the bus home thinking about her achievement and was happy but this was tinged with annoyance. How unjust is it that showing emotions like passion or tears was looked upon as anger or even worse thought of as a sign of having mental health struggles! "Why was there such a stigma associated with mental health struggles anyway?" was a question she asked herself.

Sophie continued with her progress and attended a women's centre that the psychotherapist had referred her to and this was one of the first places that she had truly felt safe and where she did not feel judged. At the centre she embraced trying new things, she joined art groups where she rediscovered her love of drawing and found that water colour painting was so relaxing. She had a form of healing – a thing that she had heard of but never felt comfortable to let a person be so close to her especially as the lady suggested closing her eyes. The lady had very relaxing sounds playing and Sophie laid on a bed, the lady put strong smelling oil on her wrists and at first she felt herself feeling very uncomfortable but after a few minutes she found herself drifting and as the lady put her hand over parts of Sophie's head and body she felt a warmth she had never felt before.

Sophie built herself up at the women's centre and wanted to give back so she became a peer mentor and would support others in the hope of being able to give them faith. She wanted others to see that they were cared about and that they were not alone. She knew exactly how alone they could feel as she herself had been there. It felt good to Sophie to be able to guide others and offer the support that she had wished was there when she started her journey.

It was at the art group that Sophie met a lady called Hope. She came in quietly, almost like a vapour. That day the art group was going to be using pieces of broken tiles and glass to create an art piece. It was to be inspired by

Kintsugi which is the Japanese art of repairing broken pottery.

It holds an important message to stay optimistic when things fall apart and rather than give up on things, to embrace and celebrate these things which also applies the same to life. Even where there are broken areas in your life you can nevertheless find beauty as they are all pieces of you. Instead of throwing away a broken object, the Japanese repair it with pure gold making a feature of the broken area. This makes the object even more valuable and beautiful despite what has happened to it.

Sophie sat next to Hope and they talked together about the part they were creating, choosing the pieces they were putting into their design. They worked together and had a cup of tea while they worked.

Sophie had reached a point where she was happy to share her life story whereas Hope didn't seem to want to share. She was happy listening and spoke mainly of her own past love for creativity. Sophie told Hope about the places where she had found support and compassion from others. She had wished someone had been there to tell her when she was all alone and felt hopeless. Hope really listened.

Both Sophie and Hope sat back at the end of the group and smiled at each other. The sun was shining through the window and was glistening on their creation. What was at the start merely a pile of broken bits was now a very colourful art piece with beautiful colours and shapes throughout.

The group leader praised them for their creation and asked if she could display it at the front of the centre so it could greet everyone who came in. In her words it gave her the feelings of 'peace, calm and happiness'. Both agreed.

Art group finished. Before she left the centre Sophie went to the bathroom where she saw Hope checking her make up in the mirror. She had a very distant, wistful look on her face. Sophie chatted a bit more to Hope. They walked out together and stopped in the foyer to look at their Kintsugi creation before they left. Sophie felt drawn to give Hope a big hug. As the two left they both smiled at each other.

The next week Sophie did not see Hope at the women's centre. When she got there another lady said that Hope had left an envelope for her. Inside was a small, pink piece of the broken tiles they had been working on the previous week. It was shaped like a heart. A small piece of paper was also inside. Hope had written "Thank you" and two kisses.

This made Sophie smile, she tucked it into her pocket. She prayed that Hope's journey would take a positive turn.

Sophie continued on her own journey. She was discovering things about herself that she had not addressed and things from her childhood that she had buried deep down. While there were many tears it was in most a cathartic experience to finally be able to open her heart to them.

With the new found openness came confidence! She did face many knockbacks as she still had a naivety where she saw the best in everyone and some of these people would see that as weakness. Sophie began to feel interest again in her passions that she had locked away within her emotions for so long.

With all of this came a determination to fight with every breath to see her children more and to fight to clear her name for her voice to finally be heard. She made a promise to herself that instead of metaphorically beating herself up for what she saw as her failings she was going to use them as growth and like the Kintsugi art creation that Hope and she had made she would stay optimistic and celebrate her flaws.

When her nightmare started all Sophie wanted was to get back to the old her and the frustration at losing herself had been a sticking point but finally, she saw that the 'old her' was past. She was now ready to embrace who she had become and she discovered she liked the new her. She now looked in the mirror with a smile and a new found confidence.

She no longer hated the reflection looking back at her. She embraced how much she had put in to get to where she was now and while her journey had not finished, she was making strides in the right direction, seeing beauty in what was once a very broken her. After all her name was Sophie and that name, given to her by her grandmother, derived from the Greek word which meant 'wisdom'.

What started as an invisible voice became a very loud, strong voice that was going to be heard.

Chapter 13

A strange lady is looking at Hope. The lady is wearing huge heart shaped, iridescent sunglasses. "Those sunglasses are weird," thinks Hope. It wasn't just the sunglasses that stood out. The woman had a happy confidence that seemed to warm the air. With her bright red lipstick, pink woolly scarf, bright green overalls and short cropped white hair she made an impression sitting against the grey stones of the Cathedral.

The woman looks intently at Hope and smiles at her. "Why is she smiling at me?" The lady quickly beckons with her hand. Hope turns to see who she is motioning to but there is no one else around. She raises her eyebrows curiously and walks hesitantly towards this strange woman. What does she want from her?

It is a sunny day with the bluest of skies. As Hope approaches the woman, she looks down into her face. The sunglasses refract the light. Hope sees herself mirrored in the lenses. There is a dazzle of light.

Chapter 14

Hope is standing in front of an open door.

What makes a place inviting? In the past, Hope has stood at the edge of a doorway and felt the bad, stale air and knew it was a place where you get slapped or crushed. Where secrets are no more and betrayal is just out of sight. A television show blares in the background. The presenter shouts over voices of families at war. They shoot their ammunition at one another, eyes raging with mistrust and pain.

In that house bottles of spirits line the counter. Most of them empty. Like a kid showing off their trophies on a bedroom shelf. Here is the relentless thirst for forgetting. And you walk in, breathe in the war and the hurt and the lostness. The bottle hits your lips and you can forget the whole sorry mess.

But this was different. As she stepped towards the open door, she feels the pull of light. The mat lying at the door speaks the welcome. Something lovely and generous is

drawing her in, like an Italian woman stretching out her arms to gather her washing in. There can be no resistance to the force of those arms because she knows how to love. Shirts, some faded overalls, a pink mini skirt, various types of underwear, a baby's soft yellow dress, socks of all sizes and worn jeans flutter happily over the narrow passageway. Each item signals who lives here – a toddler, a young woman, definitely a baby, an old grandad or maybe it's a father. Each yank and pull draws them in closer to her. And that feeling, that image draws Hope forward.

Chapter 15

Year: 1991
Penny's story

Initially, Hope tries to peer around the door. She steps carefully over the threshold then slowly moves past the door into what appears to be a converted pig stye.

The kettle is boiling on the table next to where she is standing. Hope is in a large, beamed room. There are a number of chairs around the room and bean bags on the floor. A warm and welcoming sense is everywhere. The chatter of women can be heard like a soft song. A comforting hum is all around her and flowing through the room. The women's song is like a choir hushing their voices, aware they must conserve the power in their lungs to build and belt out the finale. A large stuffed owl is in a glass case. There are a few women sitting in the chairs holding their babies but most of the women are heavily pregnant, some standing, others walking through the room.

Where am I?

A quote on the wall written in beautiful calligraphy says, *"I will not simply survive I will Love."*

The room seems to represent many life times that mothers have been in this situation. A beautiful short haired blonde woman comes into the room. She looks ethereal like an angel. Hope approaches this woman. She asks who she is.

"I am Selma, an active midwife."

"What is that?"

Selma explains, "I deliver babies naturally."

Hope can see that Selma is a kind and delightful person. She is highly attentive and very intelligent. She is considered to be ahead of her time.

Selma had been convent educated. The nuns encouraged her because they could see that she had dexterity and confidence. She related well to others. Selma always honoured her friends. She married and had a good husband. He was a scientist. They had met at university.

Selma had a dream to enlighten mothers about their active responsibility in birth. Before women didn't have choice. Lying on back, legs in stirrups and "now push". There were no choices.

After she left university, Selma had gone to Africa for greater experience. She learned so much from the African mothers and the midwives who helped them give birth. She learned traditional methods. Compared with England's sterile and cold rooms where mothers would lie on their backs. "It is against gravity but easier for the person delivering." Selma shook her head.

Selma returned to Britain with a dream to provide a safe place for women to have natural birth and choices for them and their baby. She faced so many obstacles as a midwife. Doctors treated her as an irritant. Their attitude seemed to be that what they did was 'professional' work whereas midwives were somehow less than. She remembers at the beginning of her career she borrowed some surgical gloves without asking. It was an emergency. However, she was rounded on by a consultant who reprimanded her like a naughty girl.

"Can I ask a question?" Hope asks.

"Of course," says Selma.

"Why do you have an owl in that case over there?"

"One very cold winter's morning I went into the barn outside. Lying on the straw was the owl. She had died. I had not realised she was hungry."

Selma kept the owl as a memory to always make sure she cares for all around her.

Selma explains, "Pregnancy is marvellous but can also be dangerous. The body will have gone through immense challenges while creating a new human being. It also must sustain this new little creature until the time of birth. Did you know after the placenta detaches from the wall of the uterus it leaves a wound the size of a dinner plate inside each mother?" Hope says she didn't know this. "What you have been through would have been very traumatic for you not just physically but emotionally. Did you get any help for all the trauma you suffered?"

"No, nothing. I just had to get on with life. There were meetings and going to court and of course I needed to go to the centre to see Archie, my son. I got to see him three times a week for two hours. But a few weeks later the social worker said Archie was unsettled after contact so it needed to be reduced. No one seemed to think he might be unsettled because he was regularly being taken away from the voice and smell of the one who carried him for nine months. Or that his mother was in immense emotional pain and anxiety."

Hope goes on to explain. "A stranger would bring him in their car and drop him off each week. He would be collected by that stranger to be taken back to my ex and his wife, Vicky. The stranger might be a different person each week. What child would not be unsettled by all of this? Archie was hearing my voice, smelling my scent and the heartbeat that for nine months that had been his world. Their answer was for him to see less of me.

"I was frantic to do anything I could to show I could care for Archie. Whether it was attending a domestic abuse programme or AA I was willing to do anything. A psychiatrist and psychologist were booked to see me. I couldn't sleep at night. I kept worrying about Archie. Was he ok? Were they getting up in the night? Who were the people caring for him? Would anyone listen to me? Would anyone help me? I knew people were looking at me. I was pregnant. Now I am not. Where is the baby? It was a dreadful time. Plus, I was still trying to see my other two kids.

"They gave me a leaflet about the contact centre which came in the post. It set out what expectations social services had and what I could expect. It was written in the most formal language and made me feel even more anxious. I remember feeling like I didn't matter. It was headed 'DEAR SERVICE USER'. Who calls other people 'users'?"

The letter said:

You can expect us to be on time and to ensure your child is brought to the centre. We will not be discussing your case during contact.

We expect the following from you:

'Dress appropriately'

There is nowhere for you to wait. Please do not turn up earlier than the stated time.

The contact supervisors should not be subjected to abuse. If they are, contact will be stopped and you might not be able to return to the centre.

Focus on your child.

...and other sentences that make you feel cold, unwelcome and unwanted.

Hope wonders where the kindness was in all of this. Why couldn't the leaflet be worded like this:

Dear Guests

Do come in something comfortable. There isn't a lot of space at the centre so if you arrive early there is a coffee shop across the street. Let us know you have arrived and we will be ready to welcome you 5 minutes before the start of contact.

You may be going through a very tough time right now and things are probably very stressful. However, we want your time with your child to be enjoyable. Let's work together so that everyone feels safe and cared for. We know there will be lots of things you might be worrying about so do ask questions once the children aren't in the room. We will try our best to answer them. If we don't know the answer, we will try to point you in the right direction of who might know.

Hope feels safe enough to open up about what happened at court. "When they placed my baby, Archie, with my ex I was devastated. He and his wife kept Archie for four months but then they found out that they were expecting their own baby. They decided they wouldn't be putting themselves forward to care for Archie after all." Hope fights back tears.

"I felt at last this was my chance to get Archie in my care. I tried so hard to convince the Judge that I had the ability to care for him. I went to all the appointments. I attended every programme they told me I had to go to. I stopped drinking and joined AA. But I was living in constant fear. I cried at some point every day. The social worker highlighted that I was emotionally fragile and could appear unstable at meetings, as I often broke down when they started talking about Archie. At times I stormed out of meetings. I just couldn't cope with the pressure.

"Who could ever imagine going through all that alone? No one else had any idea of what I was going through. Court on top of it all was horrendous. The barristers and social workers and the other lawyers would all gather in a side room. Sometimes I could hear them laughing or talking about the best place to get lunch. I wanted to scream at them all, '"my baby has been taken from me!"

Selma explains that after a woman gives birth their cortisol levels and hormones take a long time to regulate.

The adjustment emotionally for any new mother is significant. "It seems that no one was considering the distress you were going through."

"They were certainly considering me but not in the way you are thinking. I attended the appointments to be assessed by a psychologist and a psychiatrist. Everyone wanted to find out *'What was wrong with me?'* No one seemed to really take into account what had happened *to* me and what *was* happening to me! The response to what was happening to me and what had happened to me was that I was a problem that needed fixing.

"No one saw my distress as a normal response to what I was experiencing." Hope takes a deep breath, "I think most people would behave in a way which might not be viewed as reasonable when going through trauma and high stress situations, yet my reactions were placed under a microscope. I felt pitted against social services who were doing the 'examination' and they felt justified in asking me the most personal questions that no one would dare ask anyone on their first meeting. 'Tell me about your childhood. When did you first become sexually active? When you were raped? How did it happen? Who did you tell? Are you sexually active at the moment?'

"The psychologist reported that I had a borderline personality disorder and struggled with dysregulation of my emotions. I was told I needed a type of intensive therapy for at least twelve to eighteen months. Of course, no one would pay for that. They said Archie couldn't wait until I could get the therapy (the therapy that no one would pay for) and that there were no guarantees it would help me anyway. The report stated his timescales couldn't wait. The timescales of being forever severed from his mother?

"Could anyone know how it would all look when Archie was eight or eighteen years old? The court considered there was a likelihood of emotional harm. It ultimately meant a life without me, his mother." She pauses. "He was adopted."

"I wrote about a poem about it. I found it the other day." She pulls out a crumpled piece of paper from her jacket pocket. "Would you like to read it?"

Selma face is filled with kindness as she smiles at Hope. "I would love to read it".

Selma takes the piece of paper and begins to read softly:

The darkness delivers no rest.
Will they remove my baby ?
Can lawyers mould my words to their will?
A crest of the lion and unicorn rests above the judge's head.
Look, even they turn their heads away.
The man in the wig says my child needs a 'true mother', a forever home.
In truth, I am his mother. My arms are his home.
The eyes of the witnesses roll like waves.
They watch and talk about me as if they had been there.
Words flow over my head and I am cut off.
A mother's voice is hissed through the teeth of men.
I am called to the stand.
The lawyers hurl questions at me like stones.
And I need tissues because my sleeve is not enough.
Believe me, I have the heart of a Queen.

Chapter 16

As Selma reads the poem, Hope's mind drifts back to standing in the witness box on the third day of evidence.

She had arrived later than expected, having caught a train which was delayed. Her anxiety was through the roof. The security officers used their wand to check her over and told her to go to the second floor. She pushed open the double doors and approached a desk where an older man sat with a clipboard. Her voice was lowered as she asked if she was in the right place for her hearing. The usher nodded, "This is the place." Hope looked around to see a waiting room filled with people. Who were all these people? Were they all here because their children were being taken away?

She sat down in a chair and got out her phone trying to distract herself. A barrister came through the door and went to the usher's desk who motioned in Hope's direction. Then the barrister walked up to her.

"Hello, I am Mr Peters, I am here to represent you today. Would you come with me so we can chat about your case?"

"Yes, but where is the barrister who was with me last time?"

"Ah yes, at the Issues Resolution Hearing. Well, unfortunately, she has gone part heard and won't be able to represent you.

"But she knows all about my case. I had a conference with her. This isn't…"

"You don't need to worry. I have read all the papers. I am very prepared to cover this case. Didn't your solicitor contact you to let you know?"

"Well, no, I mean I ran out of credit a few days ago so I…"

"We need to go through your statement. The Judge will be calling us on shortly. We don't have a lot of time."

They went into a bare room that was stale and airless. The barrister asked her numerous questions about her statement and the evidence of the local authority.

"But the other barrister knew all of this!"

Her eyes were fixed on the man's suit, the wide pinstripes of navy, the clicking of his pen, the hard plastic desk between them and the blinds blocking out the world outside. There was a clatter as the door opened abruptly. The usher said, "Your case is being called on." The barrister gathered up the papers and several lever arch files. Hope stood to her feet as nausea swept over her. Her mind told her, "This is all going terribly wrong."

Hope sat through two days of evidence. The social worker was first. Listening to her was hard. Archie had had three different social workers from the outset of his birth. This latest social worker, Bethany, had only met Hope a handful of times. Each time they met, she seemed pressed for time, often looking at her watch and was stressed. She rarely ever returned Hope's calls. Hope learned she had twenty-one other cases to manage. Bethany made it clear she was not Hope's social worker, she was Archie's and secondly Hope needed to keep in touch with her solicitor if she needed updating.

Hope could sense that Bethany was probably well intentioned. She wasn't unkind, she just had a job to do, forms needed to be filled in and there was not enough time to even begin to know her. This woman had had training to do her job and no doubt to do it with compassion. But there was no trust and no programme would fix this. Time is what was needed and no one had much of this except Hope.

Despite good cross examination, the social worker would not shift from her position that Hope posed a potential emotional risk due to her past. Everything was about her past. What about 'the now'! The social worker parroted out a line "the best predictor of future behaviour is past behaviour." Does that mean there are no second chances? Does that apply to social workers as well?

The psychologist and the psychiatrist gave evidence. Frankly, Hope couldn't remember a lot of what they said. It was all about future harm and the ability for her to change based on their informed opinion. But she had only met them on one occasion for less than 3 hours. She later heard whispers that one of the experts had been involved in nefarious activities. Did anyone foresee that?

She heard her name being called and went alone towards the front of the courtroom to the witness box. When her feet stepped into the box her legs almost gave way. Steadying herself, hands on the cold plank of wood she took a deep breath. Her name was on the massive lever arch files resting on slope of the witness box. "If this was entirely enclosed it would be a coffin," she thought grimly.

She was asked if she wanted to swear on the Bible.

Taking hold of the book in her right hand she quietly read the words on the card in front of her, "I swear by Almighty God that the evidence I give shall be the truth, the whole truth and nothing but the truth." The Judge says, "You are free to sit or stand." Hope pulled out the foldup seat. As she sat down her head only just peered above the wooden balustrade.

Her barrister explained that Hope would need to keep her voice up as she gave her evidence. "Just face the judge and give your answers to her. She will be taking a note of what you say so keep an eye on her pen."

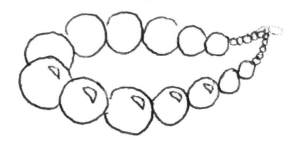

Hope stared at the silver pen held between the perfectly manicured nails of the Judge then glanced up to look at the woman who would decide Archie's and her future. She had short brown hair that frames her face, a large pearl necklace draped around her long neck and a black robe that seemed far too big for her body. The pearls were as white as the woman's teeth. Between the pen and the pearls Hope was lost in thought. The Judge's face was turned down towards the files in front of her and seemingly unaware of Hope's presence she appeared deep in thought. "Will she give me a chance?" thought Hope.

The Judge looked over at Hope but returns her gaze to the notebook in front of her and scribbles something down.

Her barrister stood in a long row in which there were three others all looking to the box. One represented the Local Authority, one for Jimmy, one for Archie's Guardian. Behind them, a second row of other lawyers also looking and taking notes. More pens, more words to be captured and snared. All she wanted was her baby back. She hasn't killed anyone. She never even threatened to kill anyone although she accepted she thought it plenty. Yes, she made a very stupid mistake getting drunk and going to Richard's house with the penknife but she was never going to use it. She was angry and drunk...

Her barrister asked Hope to give her full name to the court. Then the questions began. The morning is spent being asked about her statements made to a different lawyer, her solicitor.

"Explain to the Court what happened on the morning of March 4th." Hope looked at the Judge's pen. She didn't want to talk about that. It had been over ten months ago. Couldn't everyone see she had changed? A succession of questions flowed on and on.

The barrister asked her to explain about her present accommodation. "It is one bedroom and you accept it is not appropriate for you and Archie, Yes? Please tell the court what you are doing about that."

"Yes, well I am trying to get a two bedroomed place..."

The Judge interrupts. "Let's stop there. We will have a break for lunch and come back at two."

Hope was not allowed to speak with her barrister because she was in the middle of giving evidence. "Go get some lunch." But how could anybody eat? They say that prisoners on death row get to order whatever they like on the final morning before they are executed. Hope wonders whether they do actually eat that meal. Instead, she went outside for a fag standing next to the great brick building in which justice is meted out day after day. She wondered if perhaps they hadn't become weary of it all.

She heard the various lawyers chatting about the cost of the car parking. There was no one to talk to and no end to the fear gnawing at her. With a strong coffee in her hand, she waited. Jimmy tried to get her attention at the corner of the building. She quickly went into the security desk to be scanned. She hated him almost as much as she hated herself.

They were called back into the courtroom and Hope returned to the place in the box. The cross examination started and carried on until the end of the day. The shattering of her sense of self was on display for everyone.

She has blocked most of it out except the worst part.

The lawyer for the local authority went through the incident when Jay and Maddie were harmed. The barrister's voice became raised and her piercing eyes were boring into Hope. In determined and precise details, she takes Hope through that night and the following two days. "You didn't get help for your children, did you? You knew they had been injured and you did nothing. You keep making excuses and it's everyone else's fault, isn't it?" She brings out photographs of the children's injuries and asks Hope to look at them. No one drew attention to the photographs of the welts and bruising on her body.

What she did was wrong. No one had to tell her that. If

she could turn back the tide, she would. She desperately loved her children. She was a good mother. She failed on that occasion but everyone can change, don't we believe that?

"Any course – I will do it. Any therapy – send me and I will go." But no one would forget what happened and her past and that she had no support. The wound in Hope ached and swelled and the pen kept moving.

Chapter 17

She feels Selma's arm around her shoulder. She says softly, "I can't imagine what you have been through. I am so very sorry."

"Lately I have been coming to realise that my love for Archie and Jay and Maddie can never, ever be destroyed and I can be proud of that. I am starting to think that I want to heal and find a way forward. I want to move forward despite the pain."

Selma says, "Hope, that is wonderful. You have been hurting so much. I am glad you are choosing to find healing."

"But the thing I struggle with more than anything else is the anger," says Hope.

A beautiful woman with jet black curly hair enters the room. Selma tells Hope that this young woman is due to give birth in three months' time. She is a single mother from St. Helena in Africa. She came to work in the UK and fell in love. The man disappeared despite making many promises to her of his undying love. Selma explains that this young woman feels a fool for allowing herself to be led into this situation. She had had a great education and a future ahead of her but now she feels afraid and ashamed. Her ancestry and history in St Helena were very moral and now look at her!

Selma adds, "I think maybe you could help her. Come with me. I want to introduce you to her."

Selma and Hope walk towards Felicity who is seated in a big wicker chair. The back of the chair fans out behind her like a peacock. Felicity has a hand resting on her swollen belly and smiles brightly. Hope understands more than this woman could realise of the pain of rejection and betrayal. She looks at her sitting in this majestic like throne and wants to put her arms around her and cry. The path ahead is hard but she will survive. Hope wants her to know this.

Hope watches as Selma talks to Felicity. They begin to discuss Felicity's birth plan but Selma is called away. Felicity and Hope begin talking about their upbringing. Although they had such different childhoods they connect as woman to woman. Felicity is twenty-three years old. They both do an exercise together called "If I was the last person on earth I would..."

Hope says "If I was the last person on earth, I would sprinkle stardust across the world and recreate a perfect world. The world would be a better place. Life would continue in an idealistic way- the past could be re-lived and I could improve the future.

"I would be out riding in nature among the forests and trees at a better, slower pace of life with a better understanding of life. My healing powers would heal the entire planet starting with the heart of my town. Autistic people and neurodiverse people could contribute more and change the planet. That's what I would do."

Felicity takes hold of Hope's hand and holds it to her cheek. As she does so, the door opens and a volunteer walks in, bringing a tray with biscuits and tea for them both. Like a paperclip to a magnet, they are drawn to the sound of the cry of a baby that escapes from the room next door. They turn their heads and look towards the sound. The volunteer asks, "Would you like to see the baby, Hope?"

Previously Hope never liked to see or even hear babies. It just hurt too much. She would do everything she could to avoid them. If she heard a baby cry, she would look for an escape. She had to get away from it.

But today Hope wants to see this new life. She is shown to the next room where a child has just been delivered. Selma is beaming as she holds a tiny baby. Her little pink body is wrapped in a hand knitted blanket. Selma is hushing her as she rocks her gently in her arms. Her proud mother looks over at her baby as she is being washed.

Selma says, "Did you know that the DNA of every mother, her genetic material, will remain in her children all their lives?" Hope smiles at the thought of this. "Forever? Wow, that is amazing!"

The baby's little fists are balled up next to each cheek. "She looks like a mini cherub ready for the boxing ring," laughs Hope.

She marvels at the perfection and beauty of this child. Her miniature fingers are so perfectly formed. Hope steps in close to Selma and stooping down looks closely at this precious treasure. She can't take her eyes off the baby. Smiling, she moves her hand towards the little bundle. Hope's fingers gently touch the tiny fist. The child slowly unfurls her fist and her tiny hand wraps around Hope's little finger.

There is the 'woosh' of the door opening and Hope is gone.

Chapter 18

The older woman beams at Hope, taking off the heart shaped iridescent sun glasses. Her grey eyes shine and sparkle. She notices that Hope is lost in thought. "How are you, Hope?"

Shading her eyes and looking at this woman, Hope asks, "I'm sorry, but how do you know my name?"

"I wondered if you didn't remember me. The last time you saw me was when you were thirteen years old. I used to run Lavender Farm."

Hope takes a step backward. "Oh my gosh! Fran! How are you? I am so sorry. I didn't recognise you. What are you doing in Edenton?

"I just moved here last year. The farm is now run by people who can look after it better than me."

"Well, I don't think anyone could run the farm better than you. It was always my most favourite place to go when Nanny Jane could have me stay. Do you remember the Victorian Day at the farm when I came with the holiday club? I think I was the only one of the 'Victorian' girls wearing a Christmas apron and a bobble hat!" Hope laughed remembering it.

"That was your Nanny Jane for you!" Fran looked tenderly at Hope. "I heard she had passed. That must have been really hard for you."

"Yeah. I was twenty-one years old when she died." She

paused, "I still miss her." Hope chokes back the emotion. Just thinking of Nanny Jane and the loss always made Hope feel this way.

"Of course you do. My husband died last year. I know I will never stop missing him. How to keep going without them is the hardest part."

"I am so sorry for your loss. Is that why you moved to Edenton?"

"Yes, partly. It's a long story. It is taking time to feel settled. I miss Cornwall, the animals and the farm but this is a new beginning. I guess we can all have new beginnings even at the age of seventy-one!"

"Are you seventy-one? Really?! I hope I look that good when I am your age."

"Oh, you are a sweetie! I am trying to keep my fitness up but it's a big battle."

Just then there is a ping on her phone. Fran says, "Oh. I need to go. I have a dog at home so I had better get back to her."

"Of course. It was nice meeting you again after all this time!"

Fran struggles to get to her feet. Hope notices a walking stick. "Oh no! Have you hurt your leg?"

"Well, I had a little accident. Nothing serious. Just means I need to give myself more time to get to where I need to go!"

Seeing a large bag of shopping, Hope says, "Let me walk you back to your place. I can carry your shopping."

"Oh, that's so kind but it's quite some way."

Hope insists, "No, please let me."

"Well, if you don't mind, that would be such a help."

Hope's face beams. "I really want to. I have nothing going on today...like most days."

Hope walks down cobbled streets with Fran then heads up past the market to the flat. She is glad she offered to help. She can see Fran is struggling to keep her balance.

When they arrive, Fran opens the door and a gorgeous, reddish brown cocker spaniel comes bolting out the door, bounces up in the air, spins around the two women like a whirling dervish and then sits abruptly on Hope's foot!

She is totally adorable with a big fringe of hair covering her one eye. Hope reaches down and gently strokes the dog whose tongue is hanging out of its mouth, its head cocked upwards and its eyes firmly fixed on Hope.

"Meet Jazzy!"

Hope is smitten and chuckling. "What a lovely dog! How long have you had her?"

"I got her after David died. She's been my buddy this last year. I don't know what I would have done without her, actually. I just feel bad that I can't give her the exercise she really needs."

Hope's voice rises. "Maybe I could walk her sometimes?"

Fran's eyes lit up. "That would be amazing, if you were up for it. Just know this, nothing, but nothing tires her out. You will be exhausted before she even starts to show the slightest sign of slowing down."

"It would actually really help me. I am starting to try to

get out of my flat more and I struggle with sleep so maybe she will help me too. Wear me out a bit!"

Fran looks at her with compassion. She is aware that Hope's life has not been easy. She doesn't ask any questions. "Why don't you come around on Sunday. You can take Jazzy out and I will cook us a nice roast for when you get back."

"You don't need to do that. I am happy just to walk her."

"I love cooking and I have no one to do it for. It will be my pleasure!"

Hope leaves the flat walking on air. She feels a skip in her step and can't wait until Sunday comes around. As she turns the corner, she sees him just ahcad of her on the other side of the street. Ducking down beside the parked car she feels sick. She crouches lower, her heart pounding violently, leaning her head against the side of the car she tries to calm herself. "Why is Jimmy on this street? Did he see me?"

She lifts her head slowly to peek out of the driver's window. Her eyes dart rapidly around trying to see where he has got to. Suddenly she hears a noise next to her. She jerks her head up and sees her reflection in the wing mirror and she is gone.

Chapter 19

Year: 1891
Dani's story

Hi, I'm a little girl called Caroline. I was brought up on a poor farm in the Victorian times.

We had a few goats and pigs but I had my favourite – my horse called Zulu. She was grey with blue eyes, and dark speckles of black on her coat. The black was blacker than a crow. She was taller than me. I had got a lot of growing to do to catch up with the height of her!

Zulu came onto the farm as a foal as nobody wanted her because she was the runt. My parents said I could have her to look after but I believe the reason they only give her to me was because they didn't think that she would outlive the life that she came to have. That's the only thing my parents ever let me have in my whole life living on the farm. I valued that horse and I told her everything; all my little secrets.

Growing up in the Victorian days wasn't easy. At times we didn't always have clean clothes as mum and dad are busy on the farm. The women lived in petticoats, bodices and full skirts. As for food on the table to eat, well we didn't always eat everyday – as there just was no money to buy it.

We lived in a crumbling, stone cottage which was shared with Grandpa and Nan. There was never ever any

work done to it. If anything went wrong it stayed wrong. There was never any heating. It was always cold and had damp. It was nevertheless a pretty cottage but it was crumbling due to it not being cared for.

It wasn't a happy time, my childhood. My grandparents were old and poorly. I saw things I should have never seen as a child. My father would beat me if I did something wrong and not feed me that day. My mother was a very quiet person, who was very scared of my father; scared to say 'boo' to a ghost. My childhood was very sad and lonely.

I remember that I just would go see Zulu and the other animals for comfort. When I would talk to them for company, I knew they actually listened to how I was feeling. They didn't tell me I was being silly like mum did to me. They never shouted back like my parents did if I said something out of place.

The pig was great fun. Josie was her name. I would pick apples from the trees and feed them to her. She would love them – crunching them up greedily and she really enjoyed them. It would give me comfort that she was really enjoying her food and excited to see me because I would give her treats. We had a really good bond. She knew me. Every time she saw me she would come jogging up to me cause she knew I would have an apple for her.

One day I was so low because of the atmosphere at home. I wasn't allowed to go to school because my father didn't let me. I couldn't take no more of living on the farm the way it was, especially with my father when he would beat me. So that day I took Zulu and went for a walk down the lane and just kept walking. I was sad and in tears and emotional but I knew I couldn't turn back. I didn't know where I was going. I was just going forward all on my own and scared but I never looked back.

I walked on and on. Then I met this lady called Hope.

She was wonderful to me, so kind. I met her at the end of the sandy lane around five miles from the farm. I was so scared.

At that moment, Zulu stopped in his stride. I got off Zulu and gave her a kiss. I said, "We are free, Zulu, we are free!" She just gave a grunt but then bowed her head and kissed me. At this moment a lady came up to me.

She was like "Where are your parents, darling? I was like, I have run away, I can't cope no more. I have had to run away." She said kindly, "Don't worry sweetheart, I will give you a room and I will look after you."

She was caring and kind and nurturing and she really genuinely cared about me. "What about Zulu?" I asked. Well, the lady had a stable at the back of her garden. She also had a patio in the corner on the right side and a long-shingled path to the left and led all the way around. There was the paddock at the back. It had all been redone and she was about to buy another horse but she said, "Don't worry I won't get another horse. Zulu can be the only horse for both of us."

This house was warm with a fire spitting, red and blazing hot. We would eat our meals at a round table downstairs in the living room. The atmosphere was calm and peaceful and there was no hostility. I was so happy and calm. I could think about my emotions and thoughts. I was glad I was free from abuse and neglect. I never wanted to go back and I wasn't sorry I left. I was so thankful to Hope. She was such a blessing to me.

On my birthday, I came downstairs, there was a great big steamed pudding on the table ready to eat. I was anxious but excited to eat some proper food. Usually on my birthday I would get nothing. I would be lucky if I even got a meal but here on this day Hope just made it a special day and I felt truly honoured by the love.

The house where Hope lived wasn't far from the beach. Me and Zulu would go down to the beach and would have a lovely gallop along it. She loved racing on the beach. Two years later she passed away. I lived happy knowing that I had had Zulu in my life and I had been blessed with such a wonderful horse. Nothing could ever replace Zulu but I knew I had to continue to go forward with my life and make the most of every opportunity that came to me. I did it for Zulu as I knew Zulu would be proud of me. Zulu was my world. She helped me escape abuse and harm so I was forever grateful. Zulu would always be in my heart for the rest of my life.

As I grew up, I found my life completely changed. Hope helped support me with going through life events which were traumatic and helped me out of darkness and to build my confidence.

I can achieve anything if I put my mind to it!

Chapter 20

A few months ago, Hope would have only gone to the shops to buy fags, alcohol and a few energy drinks. Today she is going with a different shopping list. She lugs her body out of bed struggling to escape the duvet that has wrapped itself around her body like a fat python. Her tousled hair is still unruly but falling gently around her face. She shuffles towards the window. Reaching out she pulls back the curtains and showers her room with light.

There is a plan for today. She is going to cook a proper meal. Fran has been helping her to learn to cook things she has never even heard of. Not being very keen at the start she has, little by little, grown in confidence. Tonight, Fran and Jazzy are coming over for a meal.

Excited about their visit she sets off to the shop with her list in the back pocket of her purple tracksuit bottoms.

Outside the store there is a busker. He's got long, dark dreadlocks, sparkling brown eyes and a guitar that beats out a tune.

The words of the song catch her attention. He sings that we only see a tiny, little fraction of the universe. Yet even a tiny raindrop can reflect the whole sun.

It reminds her of a song she used to dance to alone in her room. She smiles at the guy and nods her head to him. She reaches in her pocket and feels a coin. She tosses the fifty pence piece into the open guitar case smiling. The busker gives her the biggest grin back, nods his head and plays on.

She enters the store and starts the search along the shelves. Finding all the ingredients she hauls the heavy basket to the self-service checkout. She scans each item as she hums the tune she heard outside. Her bank card is swiped but a message appears – 'card declined'. She swallows hard. Her mouth is dry. There isn't enough money for the shopping! Desperately looking into her bag, she frantically searches every pocket and lining. £4.43. That's it.

Her cheeks feel hot. A large knot in her stomach is growing. Her palms are sweating. She looks around frantically, eyes darting around the tills. She can't seem to breathe. "Everyone can see my panic." The thoughts racing, whizzing, fizzing through her mind. There is a struggle between breath and mind – how to slow down her thoughts because everything is out of control. "I need to put some things back! But I need these ingredients!"

Seeing movement above her head she looks up and sees herself in the security camera. It is capturing her panic and she is gone.

Chapter 21

Year: 1600
Janice's story

Kwame was tall, lanky, with arms and legs that seemed to operate independently of his body as if they had a mind of their own. He lived a simple but fun and amazing life with the other young people in the village, planting and cultivating, hunting boar and buffalo, and fishing. He was about a year into an apprenticeship with his father, the Master Gold Craftsman. This required a lot of skill and attention to detail.

However, Kwame's mother often voiced wearily of his heavy handiness, his ability to knock over even the most sturdy things in the house. He resembled a baby giraffe taking his first steps steady for a split second then gracefully slipping and sliding. However, he was charming, kind and had the warmest smile, with brilliant white teeth due to his obsession with using the chewing stick from the lime or orange trees that grew in the village. Each morning, afternoon and evening he could be seen happily chewing away while he did his other tasks.

Kwame's father was a tall, well-built man with a broad smile and large, brown kind eyes. His father was the Master Gold Craftsman for the region. He made the most ornate figures out of gold. He also made the heavy chains and jewellery that the Kings and Chiefs wore. He was intent on passing on his skills to his son, Kwame.

Kwame enjoyed watching and learning the smelting and moulding of the objects and how a small round gold blob could be brought to life representing a woman cooking, a man craving or an animal. Some items took months to make. His father often laughed at his attempts at moulding the gold, but day by day, week by week there could be seen to be improvement. His moulded sheep no longer looked like a three legged-stool. His figures no longer looked like they were men who had been badly injured after a fall from a palm tree, their limbs where no longer twisted or missing. He was progressing and would in the future take over from his father.

His father always seemed to have a treat for him at the end of the day. Some days it would be a special mango that grew only deep in the forest; it had red skin, and the most amazing smell and when you bit into it, the juice ran down your chin, it was so sweet it made you dizzy. In the evening his father would sit with his arms round him and tell him stories and proverbs from their ancestors. Kwame recalled feeling very content and safe when sitting arm in arm with his father. Life was good and he wanted for nothing.

Kwame's mother was petite and an extremely pretty lady. Kwame noticed that she received admiring looks from both men and women in the village, they admired her for her beauty as well as for her industrious nature. She was always busy doing something, cultivating vegetables, cooking, cleaning, sewing garments, she seemed to be good at everything she turned her hand to.

She was very firm with Kwame which was unlike the other mothers who seemed to spoil their sons and have them on a pedestal. Kwame was taught how to cook and had to sweep the rooms in the sleeping house, sometimes his friends would snigger when they saw him with the broom made of reeds, another thing his mother was good at making. His mother told him it's good to know how to look after yourself. "Yes, you will one day have a wife but you should share the work in the house. Don't be like the other men in the village," his mother would say. "Standing around chatting at the end of the day and their wives have to do everything. Sharing is an important part of family life." He would tell all of this to Hope and much more besides because she was about to enter his world.

Hope is feeling hot. She blinks in the bright sun. Everywhere is very lush and green. In the distance she sees a group of thatched dwellings, similar to a village in Cornwall where she once had had a holiday with Nanny Jane. It was one of the few really truly happy times she remembered as a child, they had spent two weeks going to the beach every day. She recalled the sand being cool and a bit damp in the morning but by the afternoon the sand was dry and so hot she had to run to get to the sea so as not to burn her feet. She and her grandmother swam in the sea that was so blue and sparkling it seemed like a fairy tale. They ate fish every evening for dinner her grandmother seemed to be able to transform a fish into the most delicious meal ever, the fish melted in her mouth with the most sublime taste that she had not tasted before or since.

So much had happened since being a child. So much she wanted to forget and bury. The pain, anguish and hurt were overwhelming. Why had her life turned so sour? It made her feel exhausted thinking about it.

She walks towards the Cornish-like village and sees a small group of people busy with various chores. A couple of ladies were making a mixture with a long stick and large bowl and pounding it up and down, taking it in turns almost like a well-oiled machine. She later discovered they were making pounded yam called fufu which was used like mashed potato, but by pounding it became glutenous.

Just then a tall young man comes up to her and introduces himself as Kwame. He asks, "What are you doing here?" She admits that she has no idea and does not know where she is. Kwame is a bit surprised as it is unusual to meet a stranger who did not know why they were here. Usually, they had come from other villages to buy gold on behalf of their Kings. The Kings and chiefs ruled each of the regions and were normally adorned with a lot of gold and often wanted the latest design or to add to their collection. The chiefs also performed the role of judges and settled disputes within the region, so it was important that they looked different from the ordinary man.

Kwame explains that Hope is in the Ashanti Kingdom [formerly the Gold Coast now called Ghana] in a small village. Hope is so confused. What on earth is going on? How is she in a country she didn't even know existed? She thinks, "It's so hot here and I need a drink," but there is clearly nowhere to buy anything.

Kwame offers Hope a seat on a very ornate wood stool

which he had proudly made a few months earlier. It had taken him a month of carving and whittling to get it right. He then gives her a large round brown container with an open hole and tells her it has water in it. The water is so sweet it tastes almost like nectar. She later finds out it was coconut water. It was so cool that within minutes she felt revived and refreshed. As was the custom when any visitor came to the village, Hope is offered food. The food is not anything she had eaten before but is very tasty. She finds the texture of the white substance very strange. It is almost like mozzarella in that it is stretchy but it has no flavour and sticks to the roof of her mouth. But when added with what she is told is called stew which is meat or vegetables with a spicy gravy it took on a new life. It was absolutely delicious.

Kwame is very curious about Hope. Where did she come from? Hope doesn't normally open up to strangers but finds it easy to talk to this gentle inquiring young man, with such a warm and inviting smile. Hope tells him about her city called Edenton. Kwame asks where her family are. She finds herself welling up with tears. 'Family' was a word she did not like to hear. her family had been ripped from her, her children had been taken. Kwame at first did not understand. "Why did you not go and take them back?" he asks.

"My eldest children are not allowed to be with me. I don't even know where my baby boy is. He has been adopted and I am not allowed to know where he lives. It is confidential, a secret" says Hope. Kwame feels himself welling up. "This is so much like my story, my family was taken, I too don't know where they are. I don't know if they are dead or alive. It was years ago and I have no idea where they are and have never seen them since."

He and Hope share with each other the large hole they feel deep inside their stomach that never seems to be filled. They also discuss the physical pain that they feel. How strange that your emotional pain leads to actual physical pain like being punched low in the stomach but it not healing and you never quite recover your breath.

Kwame can see the hurt and pain in Hope's eyes. He says, "Can I tell you how I survived losing my family?"

Hope is unsure whether she wants to continue talking about this subject. It is starting to make her stomach churn like a washing machine and she is feeling a bit nauseous. She can feel her anxiety rising and wants to get up and run away, but Kwame puts out his hand and gently lays it on her shoulder. She feels a calm wave come over her and the desire to get up and run fades away. Similar to the way the sun was gradually setting and fading behind the hill in the distance.

A calm descends over the village and it was as if only she and Kwame existed. She does not see or hear anyone else.

Kwame recounts his journey to forgiveness. "Many years ago white men came into our village. They had guns. My parents were brutally taken away."

Kwame could remember it so well. It was a typical day. Kwame had woken up as day broke and a chink of light flooded into the house through a hole where a bit of thatch had been eaten by some animal. He was usually reluctant to get up, his eyes hurt and usually one of his siblings would be pulling at him to get up and play. His father promised every time he looked up to mend it but that was about three months previously, still the light acted as a wake-up call every morning. He would smell the smoke rising from the fire his mother had lit for breakfast wafting through the house.

Kwame's village was near a larger settlement called Kumasi. The village was surrounded by a stonewall and trees although there were rarely any issues from other tribes. it always gave Kwame a sense of well-being and safety being inside the walls.

Kwame and Kofi had spent the morning fishing and swimming in the blue river about forty minutes' walk from their village. They had chosen this river as it was always teeming with the biggest fish at this time of year.

They had walked slowly through the dense forest on their way back due to the intense heat and humidity of the day making it difficult to hurry or to move more quickly than walking pace. As they approached the village, they could hear screaming and shouting. They saw smoke rising in the distance. Both young men were alarmed at the realisation that something was terribly wrong. As they ran to the entrance of the village what met their eyes can only be described as chaos and carnage. Some of the village houses were on fire, there were several villagers laying on the ground all injured, some writhing in pain, others still and not moving.

There was so much chaos that Kwame did not know where to focus. It was a horror scene. He scanned the scene looking for his relatives, in particular, his mother and father. His father was nowhere to be seen, but he saw his mother being dragged away by two men with guns. She was crying and looked terrified, he noticed a large gash on her leg.

He and Kofi hid in the bush for around five minutes, then he noticed that Kofi was standing up and moving towards the village. Kwame was torn. He felt he should be going to rescue his mother but at the same time, he was terrified he had no idea who these people were. He had heard rumours of slave traders that came suddenly and burnt and pillaged villages and took away the inhabitants, but he could never have imagined the sheer terror of witnessing it before his own eyes. Being rooted in fear and not being able to move despite wanting to rescue the two people he loved most in the world.

Kwame was not sure how long he had been in the bush; he must have passed out as when he woke up the sun was setting and it was getting dark. Many of the houses were smouldering now, just whiffs of smoke here and there. He was not sure if he had had a bad dream but when he finally came out from hiding, the reality hit him hard, just like when he had fallen out of a palm tree a few months back and landed smack on his face. It was if he had been physically assaulted. Wave after wave of pain and disbelief hit him at what he had witnessed. He searched for his parents and uncles and aunts, there was no sign of any of his relatives. He also looked for Kofi but he was not in the village either.

In the days that followed Kwame descended into a deep abyss of pain, grief, regret and recrimination. He literally felt like his insides were being ripped out. He had never felt pain like this before, not even when he had had three weeks of sickness and delirium after being bitten by mosquitoes. The days went by in a haze. There were just six people who had survived and were left in the village out of about one hundred and sixty originally. They soon realised that it would not be possible to run a community with just six of them. How would they do all the necessary tasks? Planting and harvesting, house building. They waited about three weeks hoping that their relatives and neighbours would return to the ransacked village. But it was very difficult to survive as those who remained didn't have the necessary skills to cultivate crops or rebuild the community, plus there were just not enough of them so they agreed to leave in search of another community to join. They knew of an Akan community about two days' walk away; they had traded gold, cloth and semi-precious stones with them in the past. So the six survivors left the village. They later joined the new community and settled in but it was not going to be straightforward for Kwame.

The heartbreak, terror, internal struggles and trauma Kwame suffered led him to suffer a mental breakdown. He was unable to eat properly and lost weight which made him look very gaunt. Someone even said he looked like a dead man walking. He had difficulty concentrating so he could no longer smelt or make gold figures or jewellery. He had no pleasure in fishing and hated to see other people enjoying the ceremonies and festivals and refused to take part in any celebrations.

He had regular nightmares and flashbacks of his mother being dragged away and the carnage in the village. She was crying and looked terrified. He remembered the truly terrible things he saw. On a daily basis, he would relive the horror, he heard the screaming and crying of the other villagers, he felt the same panic, fear and pain as if it was actually happening again. Each day he grew more and more bitter and angry and wanted revenge. It was hard as he did not know who to direct his anger to. He had no idea who had taken his parents and relatives, so he often lashed out at members of the new community. This did not go down well and led to him being ostracised because of his unreasonable behaviour and outbursts which were not acceptable in Ghanaian culture. It became a vicious circle of hate and anger and isolation.

Kwame suddenly shakes his head and slowly lifts it to look at Hope. "After this, I was not coping. I was like an empty shell. I stopped doing most of the things I enjoyed like fishing and hunting and being with others. it all seemed pointless. It seemed like my life had come to an abrupt end; like the world had stopped, time stood still. I had no hope of any future. What is a future without your parents and community? I found it hard to laugh. I felt guilty that I should have any fun when I don't even know if my parents are dead or alive, if they have eaten, if they have been hurt, my imagination goes wild thinking of the worse things that could have happened to them. I did just the bare minimum just to survive and to avoid ridicule from the new village I joined. That was until the Wiseman came to the village."

Forgiveness

Kwame shares how he began to heal from the loss of his family. "A wise man, an elder, had visited the village. I saw him on a particularly bad day when I had flashbacks of my mother being dragged away screaming with blood pouring from her leg which had a large gash. I was huddled in a corner like some bereft puppy. The wise man came and knelt down beside me and gently put an arm around me and took me through a process to release my hurt."

Kwame explains the step-by-step process with Hope.

"Firstly forgiveness – forgive yourself you may have many regrets but you cannot change the past, no matter how hard you try or replay the scenario over and over again."

Kwame believed that if he had not gone hunting that fateful day, he could have saved his family. In his mind he would have fought the intruders before they got to his mother, he would have protected his family. However, in reality that was very unlikely as he could not have fought forty men with guns, but the bereaved mind plays tricks on you.

Hope too thinks if she had not stayed with her abusive partner then maybe she would not have lost her children. if she had not listened to fear or thought she must stay with her partner for the sake of the children. If she had not listened to her friend who said "Well at least he doesn't hit you all the time" and that she should just ignore the verbal abuse and cutting put downs. But she had listened to the wrong advice and made excuses for him. That had cost her dearly. Hope also understood the feeling of time stopping, feeling worthless and traumatised beyond your worst nightmare.

Kwame explained that the Wiseman had asked, "Would bitterness and rage bring back your parents?" Those feelings bought only temporary relief, like an addict getting a fix. It's great for a few minutes or an hour but then you're back to reality and ohhh the cutting pain deep down.

"Forgiveness does not mean forgetting or agreeing with the wrongdoing, or even reconciling a relationship. You can forgive a person while in no way believing that their actions were acceptable or justified. It releases you, not them. They don't care, often they don't know that you are hurting. They can't feel it. You are the one awake at night churning and sleepless. You need to free yourself from those chains of hurt and pain."

Kwame asks Hope to describe the injustice and why she felt it was unfair. Hope tells Kwame the whole traumatic story of how she lost her children.

Secondly, Kwame tells her to think about how she is affected; the painful emotions, changed behaviour, recurring thoughts, stewing, practical costs in time and productivity.

Hope thinks long and hard and realises that she had lost years of her life in a fog of hurt and pain. The list of what she has missed or not tried grows longer and longer. Being so engulfed in grief and loss has robbed her of numerous opportunities within her grasp.

Kwame realises that his fog was one of anger and bitterness, going over and over how he would injure or even kill those who had taken his family. Sometimes he thought up the most gruesome punishment in order to get back at the people who took his parents away. At times he was horrified by the venom and hate that came up from within – he had been festering and stuck in grief

Thirdly, Kwame asks Hope, "What would be different if

you forgive? How would you feel? What would you be willing to attempt?"

Hope thinks long and hard again and her eyes light up and her face brightens. With a tinge of sadness as she realises life could have been so different if she had met Kwame earlier and chosen to forgive. "Forgiveness is a choice," the Wiseman told Kwame.

"Start by saying out loud 'I Forgive You' and the person or organisations name. At first it will feel false and may also stick in your throat but as you practice it daily, one day it will become real, and you will sense the releasing of your anger, the knot in your stomach and churning nausea will stop."

Hope says to Kwame, "I think IF I could forgive, I would feel lighter, I would be able to go out and face people and not be embarrassed by losing my children. I would feel worthy of the opportunities and offers that others have given me. I would accept whole-heartedly the opportunities and make the most of them. I would go to Contact with my children even if they were short and badly planned by Social Services. I would go prepared to Contact with as much as I could practically and I would commit to memory and treasure the smile or hug I got from my children and not be hurt and embittered that it was too short. I would remind myself that one day we will be free to meet when and how we want without interference."

Kwame tells Hope that by forgiving she will have better health, she will be less stressed, have less anxiety, and feel less hostility. She will have less depression and improved mental health.

He tells Hope, "It won't come easily, it must be

practised but when you think of how it will help and enhance your own life and the positive effect it will have when you are reunited with your children at Contact and when they are older. Hopefully, you will feel like I did and embrace forgiveness, embrace the future and fulfil your name. Hope, you deserve a future filled with emotional freedom and well-being, a future that exceeds anything you or anyone could imagine."

Hope reached out and hugged Kwame at that point they both connected and instinctively knew that they had left the past behind, not forgotten but they had forgiven. They had both found gold.

Chapter 22

By Kye

Hope knows what she has to do. She places the paper on the table and gets out her favourite purple pen.

Dear Dad

I found you through the prison service. You will probably be surprised to hear from me. To be fair I am rather surprised to be writing to you. I never once thought I would do this – maybe it proves we all can change our minds and start forgiving.

I lost so much in my childhood. At times I wished I hadn't been born but definitely I had wished for a different life. Why you did what you did will always be a mystery to me. You could have got help or you could at least left mum alone. You could also have realised I'm not my mother, I am your daughter and not blamed me for everything. But the past is the past.

For all that you took from me, you never destroyed my desire for goodness or love or forgiveness. I am starting to understand that the childhood I had is mine to accept and not fight. That is helping me to heal. It doesn't mean it was ok because it absolutely wasn't but looking back all the time hasn't worked, and carrying this inside me is much harder than letting it go.

Nanny Jane was the only person that I felt really ever loved me. She told me she often prayed to God for you. I once saw her on her knees next to the bed crying. I don't know if those tears were for me or for you. But if they were for me, they are working. Maybe it's my turn to shed a tear for you- between me and God.

You were in prison when she died. You didn't get to hear the lovely things people said about her or the crazy stories that landed her in all sorts of trouble. She was a fiery, free spirit who didn't suffer fools gladly and I miss her desperately.

The reason I am writing is to tell you I forgive you. I am not looking for a relationship with you. I don't think that is probably possible or desirable. I guess time will tell.

But I wanted to give you the chance to really hear how I feel in this letter and listen to me by reading. God hears my prayers and I thought you might want to as well.

We cannot change our families. Your blood is my blood, mum's blood is also my blood. But I am my own person. You unfortunately missed out on me and that is tough because all I wanted was your love, dad.

I don't know if you loved me. You didn't show it so I struggled to believe it, and as a child that is *hard. It is harder as an adult with all the feelings to my inner child and missed opportunity for our relationship, but it's okay dad.*

I know I love me, and God loves me too but I need to find it in my heart to forgive you. That's why I am writing this letter like I stated beforehand, to let go of the hate that I didn't cause but I can surely move on from – For me to be better and happy. From now I can start to live and love how I deserve.

I wish you all the best dad,

take care.

from your daughter

The phone is ringing. It is a video call. Fran is phoning. She picks up her mobile from the sofa and smiles, "Hiya, Fran!" Hope sees her own face in the corner of the screen.

Chapter 23

Year: 2000
Shelly's story

There are beautiful flowers all around her. The sweet smell is so intoxicating as her sweet little daisies litter a perfectly manicured lawn in front of her. It is like a fairy tale garden. A lovely fairy water fountain is bubbling away in the corner with other fairies perched on the top of a log that's built into the fountain. The fairy herself is looking satisfied with herself -filled with happiness and peace.

There are lavender hedges around a large grey villa set like a wedding cake at the top of a hill. Hope makes her way slowly up the path and she's nervous as she walks through the red, pink and yellow roses that line her way. It's like a paradise garden. She glances up to see a woman in a window watching her.

Courtney has been enjoying the beautiful view of the garden she has worked so hard with others to make. A garden like hers doesn't appear overnight. She has taken her time to plan that garden. It should be enjoyable, is what she thought and it has to be cared for as nothing grows without the right conditions. She often remarked that in 'good soil' everyone has something valuable – gifts and light to share. Courtney had succeeded in building a garden where nobody else saw anything good.

She wanted to create a beautiful garden where the women can relax and just feel safe and secure and children can play without anyone kicking off at them. She believes that in order for women to change their lives around, it is essential for them to feel safe and cared for. Some of the mothers are there with their children. Others are learning how to be good mothers with the right support around them. Peer to peer support is what is so important here, thinks Courtney.

She remembers the times they have taken the kids out to community groups and interacting with other children and women in the community. It made it normal for them not being watched with cameras and people with notepads. Even when they move out they can still return for activities with their children and help give other mums hope. Especially those that don't have confidence or a lot of family support in their lives. Those mums encourage other mothers. They show them that if they can get themselves out of difficult situations and have their children back at home then others can do it with the right help and support.

Courtney notices a woman she doesn't initially

recognise walking towards the house. As Hope makes her way slowly towards a big double door, she notices a large door knocker. It is a large lion's head. "Hmmm, how strange," thinks Hope, but she likes it as she thinks women are strong like lions.

In fact, Courtney chose that knocker as she believes women are powerful even when they don't feel like they are. Courtney enters the garden and walks down the path, approaching the new woman.

"Hi, I am Courtney. I have been expecting you."

"You have? Hope says bewildered as she has not met Courtney before.

"Yes, I had a referral from your solicitor. She said you may need our support."

"My solicitor...why has she contacted you?"

"Maybe because you need support and to get back on track with your life," said Courtney softly and quietly to Hope.

"I have tried that in the past but nothing I did was ever good enough. I am still trying though."

Courtney says, "I know. I have been there too."

Hope raises her eyebrows in surprise. "A woman like you with a lovely big house and a gorgeous garden has been through the court system?"

"Yes, it is true," says Courtney, smiling softly at her.

Hope looks directly at her with ease as she slowly starts relaxing a bit as her shoulders had been slumped over when she heard this so she relaxed a lot more and her body was not so tense.

"Why don't you come inside and have a cup of tea or something and I can explain more?"

They go inside the villa. It is decorated beautifully. There is a long corridor which leads into the kitchen. There are rooms of all different kinds leading off the corridor. Although the house is old it is modern inside. The old sash windows are letting in lots of light as it is lovely and sunny outside. As the door is open Hope can see into it. There is nice, lovely wooden flooring with lovely carpets in the rooms. A lovely, big rug is running down the large open hallway. The rug has embroidery along the sides with the words 'love, light, hope and peace' and loads of beautiful butterflies and flowers around the words. Hope feels it is nice and inspiring just looking at it.

There are many pictures on the wall of women and children. Hope wonders who are all these people. She notices a large, wooden picture framing a poem.

The GARDEN
by Donna
The petals have fallen from my rose.
I am broken.
I am put in front of others and they look at me.
They only see a broken flower.
They tell me I am weak and I cannot grow.
But I would get up every morning and sing to myself.
I will wash away the darkness.
I will dry myself with goodness, wrapping the leaves around my body.
My vines will attach to those around me.
They give me support and I am strong!
I have to have hope to keep growing.

Hope stands still reading the poem again.

Courtney puts her hand on Hope's arm and says, "Do you like it?" as she notices her staring at the poem.

"It's nice. Did a poet write that or did you get it online?"

"One of our lovely mums called Donna wrote it."

"That's amazing." Hope felt something she hadn't been able to feel for a long time – safe and relaxed and she could let her guard down. Courtney led her into the kitchen inviting her to sit down at the table as she put the kettle on to make tea.

They sit down at the large table that could seat about thirty people easily. Hope notices that the kitchen is clean and tidy and everything seems to be in its place.

"Would you like a hot drink?" Courtney asks Hope gently.

"That would be lovely. Tea with one sugar." She paused, "I used to have five sugars so I have made some progress!" laughs Hope. She laughs to herself not knowing if Courtney heard her or not.

Courtney says, "You sure have! I think it would be like syrup with five! I only have one spoon now and again." Courtney pauses, "I want to say something that may shock you, Hope. I know you. Do you not recognise me? I know it has been a long time ago but we were once together in the same place."

Hope looks stunned. Courtney does have a familiar face from somewhere in her past – but where? She shakes her head and can't place it. As Hope waits for the kettle to boil, she thinks why would this lady want me to come into her wonderful house? Hope has often felt this way because she believed she was nothing and useless and no one wanted to know her because of what she has been through in her short life. "Why would anyone give me the time of day when I have 'wrecked' my life so badly?" would often come into her mind. But this time Hope remembers that just because she thinks thoughts does not mean they are 'true' or that she has to keep thinking like that. She smiles softly at Courtney and puts her shoulders back.

Courtney says to her, "This all must seem a bit of a shock. There must be a lot of wondering going on in your head and heart."

"Well, yeah, I am wondering more than you can know! Please tell me how you know me. Were you a social worker or something?"

Courtney responds, "No. I am definitely not a social worker. I am not a professional. I am a normal mother just like yourself."

Hope is shocked, "Really?!"

"Yes, I had my babies when you did."

"What?" Hope says shocked.

"We were in the hospital ward together? I talked to you before the labour and you told me how scared you were. When the social worker took your baby, I saw you. You were left behind without him. I really felt your pain as you sat on your hospital bed crying your eyes out until the midwife came and pulled the curtain around you. I heard her say you were free to go home. I remember my heart broke seeing you without your son."

"I can't really remember much of it. I have blocked so much out because it's just too painful to remember. I really only remember that they took him away from me and never gave him back. I don't talk about it much but it cuts so deep and it is heart-breaking. I just start crying and I don't think I can stop once I start. I miss my beautiful baby every day...so, so much."

"After we met," Courtney says, "I was fighting the system for over twenty years. I never had any support myself. I was frightened and alone too until I started building trust with the right people and got support. My confidence started to grow again. I learned who was good for me and who was bad for me. Who wanted me to do well and who wanted me not do well. I learned to control my emotions and not be ashamed of what I have been through because it is part of who I am.

"I then received an inheritance which meant I could buy this amazing place. I spent twelve months getting it ready for guests. I had some wonderful friends who got involved. They helped me make it the lovely home that it is. I had a vision of setting up this place and now it is a reality.

"I took advice from solicitors and professionals so it could be like a mum and baby foster place but here it would be for mums of all ages and backgrounds no matter what their situation. We have a group here to help educate and learn the mums from other mums. In some of the groups you gain certificates in what you learn too! I can also support mums by writing letters of recommendation to the court or social workers to help mums.

"One of the things Social used against me was I didn't have a good support network around me. It's a big one they use against mums all the time. 'You have got no support'. Well, now they do. We are like one big family here. We all help each other and give each other encouragement too. We support each other to the best of our abilities and are never judgmental of each other as we are all different and unique. If a mum or yourself don't understand something we always encourage you to ask us. We all work together to help you the best we can. There is always a list of names of the mums available to offer support when needed in the kitchen on the notice board."

As Courtney drinks the last of her tea, she asks, "Shall I give you a tour of our home?"

"Yes, that would be lovely," Hope says, a bit nervous. As they both head up the large staircase with lovely curved wooden bannister, Hope can't but help notice more photos lining the staircase of mothers with their children. They seem happy too. Her mouth drops open at the sheer size of the house. It has three landings with tall ceilings and loads of rooms!

Courtney gently knocks at the first room they come to. A woman's voice says "It's open". There is a mum with curly ginger hair reading a book called 'Raindrops learn to Dance' to a child with the same bright ginger hair. They look so sweet. She smiles and says hello to Hope. Hope smiles back and says "Hi" to her. She remembers reading that book to Jay and Maddie in the past.

In the next room a mum is playing with her twins. They are laying on the floor on a big colourful crocheted blanket that was made for them. The mother is holding up a rattle to the one twin while the other has a rattle in her fist swinging it close to her brother's head. The mum says "Woah, there tiger," and gently moves the baby at a different angle so she doesn't whack her brother in the head with it. The twins are wearing baby grows that are lovely pink and blue ones which say "I love Mummy" on them. They are giggling loudly in response to their lovely mum. The mum says, "Welcome to our lovely home."

"Thanks. You have lovely babies." Hope feels hopeful and cared about too.

Hope notices there is another mum at the back of the room at a table. There are two toddlers doing some paintings of handprints with their mum. Hope goes over to look at what they are doing. She wishes she had been able to do this with Archie but she never got the chance to.

The little girl says, "Mummy I want to paint a humongous, massive sunshine with a big smiley face." Her mum nods. Hope murmurs, "that would be lovely. And maybe you could paint a big purple pony upside down too." The child laughs and says "that would be funny!" Hope tenderly places her hand on child's head and says, "Yes, it would be funny."

They hear music playing next door. The door is wide open. A joyful pop song plays from a CD player on shelf by the window. Two mums were clutching their sides laughing at each other. One is wearing cargo trousers and a mesh top and the other was teetering about on platform sandals coupled with a dress with trousers underneath. They are dancing with four kids. They kids are trying their best to teach them their dance routine but the mums keep messing it up by doing it wrong all the time. They look like they are having so much fun. Hope wants to join in too.

But the tour hasn't ended. In the last room a mum sits in a large rocking chair with her baby lying so peaceful in her arms. Just her and her baby peacefully undisturbed by anyone. Hope gently blows a kiss to the mother. The mum gives Hope the most beautiful smile and whispers back "thank you" to her.

Courtney gently closes the door to leave them, and peacefully they walk back toward the garden. "You probably forgot my story way back then. We both suffered a lot in the past. We were both going through so much heartache back then too. It is almost like a dream what happened to me. I sometimes think it happened to someone else but it didn't. It was me. I remember my twin's social worker repeatedly telling me every time I asked for help, 'I am for the child. Not you. The child is my focus.' I remember I told the social worker, 'If you care about my child, you will care about the mother.' No child wants to think of their mother being abandoned and forsaken by a social worker.

"After I received the inheritance, I could have blown it on all sorts of things but my dream was to make sure no one has to ever go through what I did all alone. I wanted my legacy to make a difference to at least one other mother." Her voice broke "And I did it."

Hope reaches out and puts her arm around Courtney. Courtney turns and hugs Hope. "Thank you," says Courtney as they hold onto each other in a tight embrace. Hope suddenly feels a tapping on her elbow. She looks down to see a little boy. "Hiya," he says cheekily. We are playing. Come Play."

Hope can see a giant game of snakes and ladders lying on the grass further down in the garden. "My mummy says would you like to play with us?"

Hope says, "Yes," but then looks at Courtney asking, "Is that okay?"

Courtney laughs and says, "Yes, of course it's okay."

Hope runs down the hill a bit towards where they are playing. She says "Hi," to the child's mum as she approaches the mother.

"Hi," says the lady. "Would you like to play a game with us?"

"Yes," says Hope, "I would, if that's ok with you. I am called Hope."

As they play, Hope feels happy. She has not felt this in years and it feels so normal as well. She wishes she could stay in this moment forever but she knows it will not last. Soon they finish their game. She says goodbye to the mum and her son and thanks them for inviting her to play with them.

As she looks round, she sees Courtney sitting on a bench just waiting for her. It was a lovely day in the garden. As Hope sits down, she asks Courtney, "Can I ask you something?"

"Why yes, of course, you can ask me anything."

Hope asks Courtney why she wanted to help other mums when she herself fought the system as long as she has.

Courtney explains if she could help at least one mum it would be worthwhile as no one else was helping them and she felt it was her mission to help in some way. She never envisioned her life to go this way but is thankful in a way that it did as she has met some wonderful, amazing people she would not have met otherwise. "If I get to help others or even one mum get her children home that would make me happy and it is all worth it – all the pain, the heartache, everything would be worth it."

As the time comes for Hope to leave, she takes

Courtney's details down and says she will think about all that had happened that day as it has been a lot to take in in one day.

"That's fine," says Courtney. "See you soon."

She waves her goodbye at the door. "Feel free to ring me anytime you need me," says Courtney. "I am always about. God bless you. Take care, Hope and I wish you well."

As Hope heads down the path, she slows down to look at the water feature with the fairies on it. There are a few goldfish swishing their tails in the pond. The sun is glittering off the pond. Hope sees a woman full of joy smiling back at her in the movement of water and... she is gone.

Chapter 24

Lying on her bed, Hope is dressed and ready to go to the women's centre but has decided to relax for a while before she leaves. Her thoughts turn to Cornelius, Sophie, the Raffs, Selma, Kwame, Caroline and Courtney. Each of them understood her. They didn't judge her. She takes a deep breath. Excited but nervous she knows the women's centre will also be a place where she will be really listened to, and not judged. She hears some girls' voices outside and smiles remembering that day so long ago when it all started to happen.

Last night she cooked the meal for Fran. That day at the tills had been distressing and overwhelming but she had managed to get her breathing under control and to ask for help from a shop worker. In the past she would have rushed out of the shop, gone home and drank a bottle of wine or whatever she could lay her hands on.

In the end, the man at the till had scanned enough to cover what was on her card and used the cash to top it up. She had to put back the parsley, the cream and two potatoes but she made do. Fran had some parsley and plenty of potatoes so it all worked out.

It's raining again, she smiles to herself. "I had better find that umbrella or I will turn up like a drowned rat!" She pulls herself up and proudly stands before the full-length mirror. She looks intently into the glass and sees a beautiful woman standing there smiling back at her.

Chapter 25

Year: 2035
Cheryl's story

Hope is on a road. She sees a woman walking ahead of her. Robots are whizzing past her. Who is this woman and what has happened to the world?!

Meeting Aaron

Emma was an ambassador for the peer-to-peer Autistic Women's group and was on her way home from the latest meeting. She helped run and host their weekly meetings.

The street was lined with electric vehicle, after electric vehicle after electric vehicle as petrol and diesel cars had now been phased out. Emma was half way down her street when she stopped dead in her tracks; it is like she had seen a ghost. On her doorstep stood a tall handsome young man in his early twenties. He had beautiful caramel skin, jet black tight ringlet curls and beautiful green eyes hiding behind a stylish pair of glasses. He was smartly dressed.

A single tear trickled down Emma's face. Emma was always terrible at remembering names but she never forgot a face. It had been a very long time but she instantly recognised the young man that stood before her. She had always hoped but never thought this day would ever come. She walked calmly towards him and as she approached him, she choked back the tears and struggled to form words with her mouth. Her lips trembled as she looked at him, asking, "Are you looking for me?" He looked at her and sighed.

Emma was still choking back the tears "I know who you are, it's been a very long time, almost twenty years." She paused. "I always hoped this day would come but never thought it would. How did you find me?"

The young man began to speak, however there was an air of disappointment in his tone of voice, "Your name is quite well known among the Autistic community. If you haven't forgotten, I am also Autistic. You were not that hard to find, but more to the point, haven't you ever tried to find me, Mum?"

The young man stood before Emma was indeed Emma's son, Aaron; he had been forcefully adopted via the UKs highly secretive Family Courts just two weeks after his fifth birthday. Emma looked at Aaron and then looked down to the floor. She looked defeated and sighed. "After all I put you through, I didn't think you would ever want to see me again and after all that you had been through, I thought you would be better off without me." She looked back up at him, "Would you like to come in for a cup of tea?"

They looked awkward just stood there on the doorstep, even more so given their Autistic nuances.

Emma said, "If you don't feel comfortable having tea in a stranger's house we can always go and get tea or coffee on the High Street if you would prefer?"

He looked at Emma, unimpressed and replied, "That would be just as awkward. Let's go inside. You owe me some answers at least." Emma lived in an ultra-modern smart home and she unlocked the door with just her voice – "Open door" – and a finger print reader. The door opened.

As they went inside, they were greeted by a scraggy old Siamese cat who was screaming like a banshee. "That's Khan. He's my unofficial therapy cat, he's very old. A few months after you were officially adopted, I had a few counselling sessions, my father and my brother passed away within months, weeks even of you being adopted and everything was weighing heavy on me. I needed the therapy or my poor old mum would be organising a funeral for another child.

"I was advised by my therapist to get a cat or a dog as they're very good for relieving stress. I found Khan in the local free ads. He desperately needed a home and he's been with me ever since – my loyal companion. I was devastated after losing you and he gave me a reason to get up in the mornings, a reason to stay alive."

As Emma led Aaron into her living room, he noticed a small elderly-looking fluffy black and white dog sprawled out on a rug in front of the fireplace, although the fire was not lit as it was a warm summer day. As soon as the little dog saw Aaron walk into the room she got up while beating her tail back and forth like she was a young sprightly puppy again. Aaron bent down to pet the dog who was very excited to see him.

"That's Luna she's very old now!" Emma exclaimed. "She has always loved people. I got her soon after I moved here. You see this was a new start for me. At my old house it was like everywhere I went there was the ghost of someone who was not dead. I could hear their laughter, I could hear their tears and could hear their final words to me over and over like one song being stuck on repeat, the ghost was the ghost of you."

Tears trickled down Emma's face. She tried to choke them back but her attempts were futile; they were flowing far faster than she could stop them.

"I thought all of these years you didn't care about me." Aaron remarked.

"That couldn't be further from the truth," Emma replied as she wiped away the tears. "Anyway, Luna has been a massive help to me and a loyal companion for many years. She helped me socialise in a place where I was alone and barely knew anyone, which is hard for anyone never mind for someone who is Autistic." Emma's Handy Home Helper 3000 wheeled into the living room holding a tray with two piping hot cups of tea and a plate of chocolate biscuits on it.

"Thank you, Mr Handy," Emma said to the robot.

"You are very much welcome Emma, enjoy your tea," replied the robot before wheeling back into the kitchen to put itself on charge.

"If you are ready to hear me out, please take a seat. It's going to be a long one."

Aaron sat down on a large black leather sofa and Emma sat on an armchair facing him. "Please continue," Aaron requested.

Emma's Story
"For you to fully understand I need to go right back to the beginning, my childhood. My father was a professional

violinist, I had an older sister Alexis and a brother called David. Due to my father being a professional musician as a family we moved around a lot when I was young as my father performed in shows all around the country and the world. The first few years of my life were great and would never have alluded to what was to come next. I will keep this as brief as possible. My father, he wasn't a very nice man, he was great until I was five or six years old and then it all started. I don't know why, but my brother bore the brunt of my father's aggression, I say bore the brunt of his aggression. My sister and I were far from left unscathed, even my mother wasn't immune from his attacks." Emma choked up and yet again tears trickled down her cheek. Aaron passed her a box of tissues that were sat in front of him on the coffee table.

"Thank you, would you like me to continue?" quizzed Emma.

"Please do, I'm listening"

Emma continued. "I guess it wasn't all bad. My father was like a Jekyll and Hyde type character. Sometimes we got the 'nice dad' but we would never know when 'evil violent dad' would appear. He could be very unpredictable and we were all always on eggshells all of the time. He wasn't just violent, he was also controlling and a bit of a narcissist.

"I think he was Autistic too, not that it excuses his behaviour but it explains it somewhat. I found myself feeling his wrath many a time. When I was six years old, he knocked me unconscious with a single blow. The reason? I was playing in a cardboard box with my sister Alexis while we were between homes packing and I was making too much noise apparently. I was six years old!" Anger could be heard from Emma's tone but she carried on. "That was the first of many blows I would experience at the hands of my father, he split my lip hurling a lever arch file at my face. Reason? I was talking too much while he was watching TV, I was around eight years old then. He smacked me over the head with a paperweight from his office bureau. Reason? Our pet dog Candy tried to steal a chicken wing off his plate so my father picked Candy up, walked to our front door and was about to strike her over the head. That is until I intervened and pushed him and made him lose his grip on Candy setting her free. He was still angry and turned his anger towards me and hit me over the head with the paperweight. It was a very heavy paperweight and it hurt, it hurt a lot."

At this point Aaron was now in tears. "I'm sorry if my story is too much for you?" Emma handed Aaron back the box of tissues.

"Thanks." Aaron sniffed.

"Shall I carry on?" Quizzed Emma.

"Yes" Aaron replied. "But you don't have to detail every event if it is difficult for you. I get the picture."

Emma continued. "Like I said earlier I got off lightly compared to my brother. While all this was going on at home I was also bullied profusely at school. I don't know if it was simply due to the actions or the idiosyncrasies of being undiagnosed Autistic maybe it was a bit of both? Things were very different back then. There was a lot of stigma attached to being Autistic. Due to girls often presenting very differently to boys we were often missed. I spent what seemed like a lifetime masking my Autism and pretending to be normal, pretending to be something I'm not.

"I met your father when I was in my late twenties, he is a few years younger than me and I fell pregnant with you very soon into the relationship and it came as a shock to me because I was always told by medical professionals that I was infertile. Although the pregnancy wasn't planned, I was very much looking forward to your arrival. When you have come from a childhood of abuse it's like what should be the best years of your life have been stolen from you and the only thing that can come close to making up for that is reliving your childhood through the eyes of your own children. I never thought it would happen and then you came along my miracle and we both know how that turned out!"

Emma burst into tears again. Aaron looked at Emma concerned and handed the tissues back to her. "Here I think you need these more than I do."

Emma thanked Aaron for the tissues then Aaron replied "You're painting me a very different story from the one I have in my adoption file."

Emma responded angrily, "Well you will soon find out that the local authority tells a lot of lies." She continued. "I didn't struggle so much being a parent when you were very young but as you got older and became more mobile my struggles became more apparent and my Autism which I had spent my whole life masking and was still masking until the day you were removed from my care. You were diagnosed as Autistic very young. I just knew you were different from other children from a very young age, you were two years old. It's not often that children were diagnosed so young back then but I pushed for it. However, as time went on, I really struggled to juggle caring for you and maintaining a home at the same time and it came to a head when I was reported by a health care professional to the local authority and they saw the state of my home and it was then that you were removed from my care."

Aaron replied "It sounds like you were having a very tough time. What happened next?"

"I put myself on every parenting course available and pushed the local authority for an Autism assessment thinking it would get me the support I needed to bring you home but instead it had the opposite effect they used my diagnosis as leverage to make sure you never came home."

Aaron replied, "I have a very different story from the local authority."

Emma frustrated, replied "You would, but they are full of lies!" She carried on "After you were adopted I quickly realised that there were a lot of neurodivergent women in the same position as me and after a lot of soul searching and the death of my mother two years ago (she left me a sizeable amount of money in her will) I decided to set up my own charitable foundation with the help of contacts I made through a local Autistic women's group where I volunteer my services every week, 'Justice for Neuro Divergent Parents.' It's an organisation I set up to provide Autism and ADHD knowledgeable advocates to parents who are going through care proceedings, we also send volunteers to local authorities to educate them about neuro divergent conditions and how to better help neuro divergent parents keep their children in their care."

Aaron looked at Emma quietly impressed. "I'm sorry to

interrupt you, it's getting late and I need to go, but I would like to meet you again tomorrow after lunch. I have a story to tell you, would you like to hear it?"

Emma's face lit up "I would like that very much."

Aaron's Story

At one o'clock the next day Emma met Aaron again, but this time at the local park. Aaron was standing by the band stand and still looked as handsome and well dressed and his green eyes dazzled in the sunlight. Red roses lined the paths and adorned the flower beds and a brass band played on the bandstand. Aaron walked towards Emma. "So we meet again?"

Emma replied, "Indeed we do. It is nice to see you again and I haven't scared you away?"

"No, nooo, not at all," replied Aaron. "When I met you yesterday, I didn't know what to expect, I half expected to be disappointed by what I found but it is quite the opposite. I was quietly impressed and would like to give you a chance to be a part of my life." Emma's face lit up and she smiled with anticipation.

Aaron looked at her. "Yesterday I heard your story and now it's time for you to hear mine! My parents, and please don't take offence, the people who raised me are my parents – Kristen and Shaun – they are good people and I have had a nice life with them. They helped me through school and university and now I am on my way to becoming a very well-respected architect at a young age."

Emma beamed from ear to ear she was very proud of her son. Aaron carried on. "I am also engaged to the most amazing woman. Her name is Zoe."

Emma watched as Aaron's face lit up. Aaron took out his mobile device a 3D hologram of his fiancée Zoe popped up. She was a stunning young woman with beautiful auburn hair and dazzling green eyes, just like Aaron's. "Oh my! She's so beautiful and I am very proud of the young man that you are becoming, you are a credit to your parents." Emma was happy and smiling but at the same time she felt conflicted and held back the tears.

Aaron carried on. "I am getting married in two months and I am inviting you to the wedding. I am also giving you a plus one so you can bring my father if you would like?"

Emma beamed. "But you haven't met your father." Aaron responded "Don't worry I have trust in your judgement. But before you get your hopes too high you will be seated with the groom's guests rather than the groom's family. I'm afraid we don't know each other well enough yet and it's only right that the people who raised me get the credit they deserve. I am sorry. I wish things were different."

Emma was happy to be invited to her son's wedding but being side-lined when it should be her in that place really stung, but she understood. "I understand, I'm just grateful to have you back in my life." Emma replied choking back tears again.

"One more thing," Aaron replied "Zoe is pregnant, it is very early days but if things go well between us, I would like you to be a part of our lives. You can't relive your childhood through me but maybe you will get to relive it through your grandchild. It takes a whole village to raise a child after all!"

Emma looked at her son while beaming. "I would like that very much."

As their walk through the beautiful park gardens came to an end Aaron and Emma said their goodbyes.

Meeting Hope

Emma looked at Aaron and beamed, grinning from ear to ear as he walked away. It was only once he was out of sight that she turned around and sobbed and sobbed into a puddle of tears. What Emma didn't notice was that the entire time she was speaking to Aaron she was being watched by a young woman in the distance. The young woman was envious of the interaction she observed between Emma and Aaron. A lovely walk with a mother and son but she was confused when she saw Emma in tears.

The young woman approached Emma concerned. "Are you ok?"

Emma replied "I am okay."

The young woman responded, "You don't look okay, I mean you looked so happy before. I envied your relationship with your son and now..." She paused. "My name is Hope. I know I am a stranger but sometimes it can help to get things off your chest!"

Emma looked at Hope. "Well, sometimes talking to a stranger can help."

Emma went on to explain. "That young man was indeed my son but up until yesterday I had not seen him for almost twenty years, after he was forcefully removed from my care and adopted through the family courts. I thought I would never see him again, until he turned up on my doorstep yesterday afternoon."

Hope butted in, "I know only too well what the family courts are like."

Emma quizzed, "Have you had children removed from your care too?"

Hope looked to the floor, and looking sad, she nodded. "They're awful, aren't they?" Emma remarked "Full of injustice! They need a massive overhaul!"

"So, if you have been reunited with your son, why are you so sad, shouldn't this be a happy time?"

Emma responded, "Oh, it is a very happy time. My little boy is getting married and he's going to be a father. I'm going to be a grandmother! I am being invited into their lives, but it is also bittersweet. As grateful as I am, I am also grieving for what should have been, for the years that I lost, for the milestones I missed.

"I should be sat in a front row seat at my son's wedding but I am relegated to 'regular guest' and it hurts." At this point tears were streaming down Emma's face. Emma continued to sob and Hope embraced her in a tight hug. Emma started to dry her eyes. "You know I have an old-time friend who always emphasises the benefits of a good hug, thank you."

Hope replied, "Sorry, I don't know your name."

"Emma, it's Emma. Thank you."

"Listen Emma, I have to go but would that good friend of yours be up for a coffee and a chat?"

Emma nodded. "Thank you, thank you, Hope. That is exactly what I need to do."

Emma pulled out her mobile device and a 3D hologram of her friend Sue popped up. "Hi Sue. I'm sorry if I have disturbed you, but do you fancy a coffee? I could do with a long chat. It will be on me."

Sue replied, "Sure, I will see you in thirty minutes". The

pop-up hologram disappeared and Emma turned around to see Hope staring in a state of shock.

"Listen, thank you, Hope for everything you did just now. I have to go and meet my friend now."

Hope said "No problem," and they said their goodbyes with a clasp of their hands. As Emma turned back to look, Hope had disappeared as quickly as she had appeared.

Emma walked into the coffee shop where she met her old friend Sue who was still very dismayed at how far technology had come. She was an older woman, twenty years older than Emma and she had seen a lot of change in her lifetime. A song from the AI Boyz, the first fully AI boy band played in the background. The coffee shop was unmanned and cashless, Sue as usual was unimpressed but she was happy to see and help comfort her friend. Emma ordered their coffees from a robot waiter and tapped her card as they sat down.

"Thank you Sue for agreeing to meet with me at such short notice. Remember many years ago when I told you I had a son who had been forcefully removed from my care? Well, yesterday he turned up out of the blue on my doorstep and – oh boy have I got a lot to tell you! Are you sitting comfortably?" Sue sat listening to Emma and comforting her with the best hugs.

CHAPTER 26

By Elina

The postman's heavy bag heaves on his side but his steps are light. Inside the bag there is a letter.

Dear Fran

The last few years have not been easy for me. It's been the worst time of my life. The pain I have been through has been unimaginable and unbearable.

I would like to thank you so, so much for helping me to get through this. It means so much to me. The kindness and compassion you have shown me is helping me to get through the darkest time in my life.

I have still a long way to go but with your help I know I can do this.

God bless you.

Hope

Help and Support

If you have been affected by any of the issues in the book, please contact:

BEAM
Email: hello@beam.support
Telephone: 01473 760800
Website: www.beam.support

Women's Aid
Website: https://www.womensaid.org.uk

Samaritans
Telephone: 116 123
Website: https://www.samaritans.org/how-we-can-help/contact-samaritan/

Family Rights Group
Advice Line (9:30am–3pm, Mon–Fri): 0808 801 0366
Website: https://frg.org.uk